I0589820

The Monster Channel

Crestwood/II Publications

The Monster Channel

Jim Simon

DEDICATION

To the guys of
The Monster Fan Club,
wherever they may now be ….

PROLOGUE

You know me. You might not have seen me yet, but you know me. I see you staring into the TV and you happen to be looking right at me, except you don't know it. I see your dull face, your glazed eyes staring at the screen. Yes, you see me ... but do not know it yet. Ah! But *I* see you. I watch you from inside the TV. I know all about you as I watch you staring dumbly at the TV screen.

You're looking right at me and you don't even realize I'm here! But I am ... I'm watching you ...

Who am I? Don't worry—you'll find out soon enough. And when you do, you'll shriek with fear.

I'm waiting for you ...

Oh, I have plenty of time to wait. After all, I can always depend on you to return to the TV ... to plunk your soft little body in front of the TV screen. Go ahead, change channels all you want. You won't leave the TV until your eyeballs are almost falling out.

And I'll continue to watch you ...

Maybe you know about this kid .... Ah! If by some odd chance you don't that story about him ... well, then, I'll tell you. You see, he was just like you. His name is Charley, and he hasn't ever been quite the same after our little encounter. And his friend—Otto is his name. Well, let's just say that Otto was always a little bit "off", but ask the local townspeople and they'll tell you it was the Creep who got to Otto, too. I kind of pushed him over the edge, if you know what I mean!

Oh, did I give myself away? Heavens!—you don't really believe in the Creep ... now do you?

You don't really believe something lives in your TV, I mean? Sure, you've seen the screen flicker and the burst of white light when you suddenly shut off the TV in the dark. You don't think that flash of light is me, now do you? Or the odd noise that screeches a little too loud when you try to adjust the volume? I mean, why would you think that's *me* calling you from within the TV ... watching you ... that is, unless you too have a Creep TV....

Oh, and did I tell you that I can control you mind, I can howl in your brain? Well, maybe I forgot to mention those things, too ...

At this moment you are probably wondering what I look like, am I right my dear friend? Well, I think I will soon be coming to see you. Then you can take a look—that is, if you can stand it! Just don't run away too quickly when

I come for you. When I come for you, I promise to come slowly at first ... after all, you see, I'm not quite the young creepy thing I use to be!

So my TV friend, continue to stare into the screen ... into my bloody red eyes. Or turn this page and read what happened to those two young fellas—Charley and Otto— when they finally made my acquaintance. I mean, what happened to those two can happen to you. And, oh yes ... don't be shy: At any time during the story you can feel free to *screeeeaaam!*

CHAPTER 1

"Welcome to Creep Town."

"What?" Charley asked the kid who had just said those words to him.

"Welcome to Creep Town," the kid repeated. The kid was wearing a T-shirt with the words ROCK OR ROT emblazoned across his shirt, and he had sneaked up on Charley, seemingly from out of nowhere. "Heck, this whole town is full of weirdoes," the kid continued. "No wonder this place is called Graves Lake Estates."

Charley said, "My parents told me this town was named after Morgen Graves, whose family used to own the lake."

"That was before you and I were born. The lake is still there, but most of the Morgen Graves family is long gone."

"What happened to them?" Charley asked.

"No one knows for sure. Some people say the family

drown in the lake during a boating accident—everyone, that is, except the youngest son, Morgen Graves. He was playing in the attic of their old house while the rest of the family was out boating on the lake. Morgen's the only one still alive today. After Morgen grew up, he built the Morgue Cable Company," the kid explained. "He owns the only cable TV company in Graves Lake Estates.

"TV is my life," Charley boasted.

"Yeah, but that cable TV company is weird. They've got this very strange cable guy. Watch out for him," the kid warned. "Of course your general run-of-the-mill not quite grade-A first-class creeps also live in Graves Lake Estates. Just look around," the kid added. "You'll see what I mean."

***

Men in yellow uniforms were walking back and forth across the front lawn of the old house Charley's parents had just bought. These were the movers, and they were carrying in the furniture.

The kid in the T-shirt asked, "Where are you from?"

"The city," said Charley.

"So that explains it," the kid said, as if he knew something special. The kid was about the same age as Charley. He held a cell phone in his hand.

"Explains what?"

"Oh, you'll see. You'll find out." The kid was nodding his head, as if he had all the answers. Then he pulled a pair of sunglasses—he called them *shades*—from his pocket. The kid put on the shades. He stared at the sun. Music started playing from the sunglasses. The kid pushed the shades up the ridge of his nose with the ball of his thumb. "By the way, my name's Otto."

"I'm Charley. Charley Nickels."

Otto slid off the shades. "Radio shades," he said pointing to the sunglasses, his eyes squinting. He folded the shades and slid them in his pocket. "In about six months from now you'll see everyone walking around with these on," he said, tapping his pocket that held the shades. "They're special. There's a little solar gizmo built into them so when the sun strikes the gizmo, it generates electricity and turns on a small built-in radio. You can't see the radio. It's hidden on a microchip, you know."

"Cool," said Charley.

"I got them from my dad. He's in what's called the consumer electronic business. That basically means he travels around the world buying and selling new kinds of electronic stuff all the time. He's always bringing home all kinds of weird electronic things. He got these radio shades somewhere over in the Far East, I think."

Otto slipped on his regular glasses. The regular glasses were black plastic with thick lenses. Otto didn't squint as much with the regular glasses. Then he took a long look at Charley's house. "I guess I shouldn't tell you this, but it's been a long time since someone lived in that house."

"It was empty when my parents bought it," said Charley.

"That's the castle of my father over there." Otto pointed at his own house across the street with the three huge Oak trees. "You'll have to come over and visit some time."

Otto was still nodding his head—he seemed to always be nodding. "But like I started to say," Otto continued, "I've got something to tell you. That's why I came over."

There was mystery in Otto's voice. Charley was not quite sure what it was, but this kid seemed to know something, perhaps a secret. A secret he needed to tell Charley.

Otto took off his thick black-frame glasses and rubbed his eyes. "I shouldn't tell you, really," he said. Otto turned and stared at Charley's house. He seemed to be staring at the upper half of the old house, the attic. "But I think I have to," he finally said. "Definitely, I have to tell you, because we're neighbors now."

"Tell me what? What's the big secret?"

He turned away from the house and looked at Charley. "I was in that house once," he admitted. "I mean, when it was empty. I climbed in through an open basement window. No one was there so I thought it was okay." Then Otto picked at a pebble. "No one living was there, I mean," Otto added in almost a whisper.

"No one *living*?"

"There was someone or something there in the house," Otto continued. "But whoever or whatever it was, it wasn't living like you and me."

"Are you trying to tell me that something dead lives in that house?"

"I know it sounds superstitious, but I saw a phantom, *the walking dead*, in there!"

Charley shuddered.

"In the attic—that's where I saw it," Otto continued. "You see, the attic door was locked but there was this kind of ancient key in the lock. So I opened it. I went up there. It seemed strange. The place smelled like old tombstones in a cemetery at night just after a rain storm." Otto kicked the pebble again. He looked uncomfortable about what he was trying to say. Then he blurted out, "I know things, you see. I mean, I know what a cemetery smells like at night because I once went to a cemetery at night with my cousin, Benny. Benny's got a car, you know."

No one said anything for a minute or two.

"*That* was scary enough to make your heart freeze up in your chest," said Otto. "I get the shakes just thinking about it. I got the same feeling when I was in your attic when I saw the Creep."

"The *Creep?*"

"It yelled its name at me. It was the ugliest thing I'd ever seen—green and slimy, with disgusting stuff dribbling out of its mouth!"

"But it's just an attic in an old house," Charley said. "An *empty* old attic. You're just trying to scare me."

Otto blurted out: "Listen, my friend, and listen well: There's this weird old TV in the attic. I was trying to get it to work. That's when it happened. That's when I saw it." He looked over his shoulder at Charley's house again. "I call it Creep TV!"

"Why?"

"—Because I *saw* the Creep come out of that old TV,

that's why!"

"You saw something, maybe. That's all," said Charley.

"Yeah, something like a walking dead man. Anyhow, I didn't hang around long enough to find out what it was." Otto's face paled with fear. "It was howling for my blood!"

"Howling for your blood?" Charley couldn't believe it.

"—It even threw something at me, something like a small rubber ball!" Otto said.

"I don't believe in dead creatures coming back to life, especially the kind of creatures that live in old TVs," said Charley, feeling uncomfortable.

"Whatever," Otto said. "Just before I ran out of there, I pulled out the TV's cable. I hoped that if I pulled out the cable, then the creature couldn't get out again. All I know is what I saw."

Otto was nodding his head again.

"Let me give you this bit of advice, Charley: If you ever see the creature trying to get out of that old TV, make sure you pull out the cable. Remember that, my friend. That's some important advice I'm giving you." Otto slipped on his glasses. "Yeah, well," he said, "I'll be seeing you. I just came over to say hello and warn you."

"What are you doing with that cell phone?"

"I almost forgot," Otto said. "That creature I told you about. If it's still in the TV, it could be dangerous to you and your family. Call me on the cell phone in case you need me."

Otto handed Charley the cell phone. "You do know how to use one of these things, don't you?"

"Sure," said Charley. "No problem."

Otto turned to go. "I've got a lot of things I've got to do right now. Yeah, really."

"Maybe I'll see you later," Charley said.

"Just beware of the attic," Otto told him, walking away. "And don't mess with that old TV."

Charley raised his hand to wave good-bye. "Nice meeting you."

"Whatever," Otto said. He was half-way across the street when he turned around. He pushed his thick black-frame glasses up the ridge of his nose and walked back over to Charley. "There's one more thing I've got to tell you."

"What's that?"

"There's a chance the Creep got out of that old TV when I ran out of the attic. I mean, I'm not sure that I trapped it back in the TV before I pulled out the cable. The attic was so dark and I was too scared to know what was really going on. What I'm trying to tell you, Charley, is that the Creep might have got loose and it could be hiding someplace in your house."

A shiver rippled down Charley's spine.

"And when I ran out of the attic, I slammed the attic door. I locked it behind me," Otto continued. "I threw that strange key into some dusty old glass jar in the basement just before I climbed back out the window. I was really shaking when I got out of there!"

"I guess that was good. That you locked the door to the attic, at least."

"Not really," said Otto. "I'm afraid that old TV in your

attic is the Creep's resting place. If it's still in your house, it will probably try to get back up there sooner or later."

The weird kid, Otto, suddenly turned and began walking away again. He was almost to the other side of the street this time when he turned around and called back, "Yeah, well, like I said before, 'Welcome to Creep Town'."

Otto crossed the street, walking under the leafy branches of the big oaks.

"Yeah. Whatever," Charley said quietly, watching the strange kid walk away. "Whatever."

CHAPTER 2

Charley Nickels was watching the movers carrying his family's furniture into the house when he heard a loud noise. It was like a bomb exploding. The explosion came from the corner of Maple Street. Charley saw a strange long black car coming around the corner there. The dark car reminded Charley of an old funeral car—a funeral hearse— he had once seen in an old monster movie on TV. In the movie, the funeral car carried vampire coffins. Suddenly the long black car belched smoke and a red flame shot out from underneath it. The creepy car crawled down Charley's street. Slowly it came, rumbling and shaking, blowing out dark foul smoke. Then the black funeral car stopped. It just sat there on the street, rattling its old iron bones in front of Charley's house. What was it doing, Charley wondered. He squinted his eyes trying to see who was driving the strange car, but he could see only a faint outline of the driver behind the wheel. The driver seemed almost ghost-like in the long black car. It was *The Thing* behind the wheel of that funeral car, Charley thought. It all gave Charley the willies. Then the black car revved its engine a couple of times and slowly drove off, leaving behind a haunting trail of smoke. From the house next door, a dog howled.

"Whoa," said Charley after the mysterious black car disappeared around the corner, "now I know what it feels like to be the new kid on the block. I'm a stranger in a strange new neighborhood!"

***

He felt a hand on his shoulder.

Charley spun around.

Standing beside him were his mom and dad. How strange, he thought, the way they had appeared suddenly from out of nowhere, like ghosts. His dad was wearing that goofy Hawaiian shirt he bought when the family went to Disneyland last summer. The shirt was blue, with parrots and coconut trees all over it. His dad had bought a shirt just like it for Charley but Charley never wore it. Charley always wore T-shirts and jeans. His mom wore her work clothes: paint-splattered jeans and a blue denim work shirt.

Before Charley could tell them about the car, his dad, pointing to the cell phone, said, "Where did you get that?"

"The kid who lives across the street gave it to me. He's letting me use it for a while."

"So you've already made a new friend, then."

His mom asked, "Do you like it here, Charley?"

"I guess so." He didn't want to hurt their feelings, so Charley didn't tell his parents that he really missed their apartment back in the city. He missed his friends from the old neighborhood. Even more, he missed The Monster Store, the place where he used to buy his monster comics and rent monster videos. That was his favorite place because it was where he got to hang out with The Monster Fan Club, a cool bunch of friends from his old neighborhood who shared his fascination with monsters. He even had a neat nickname when he hung out with his Monster Fan Club friends. He and his friends called him, Uno, Master of One. He liked that nickname because he said he was the master of his own fate. Thinking about all that made him miss his friends and the old neighborhood more than ever. Why did his family have to move to this house anyway? His mom and dad and his twin sister, Chrissy, called it their new house, but from where Charley stood on the sidewalk, it looked like a very old house. Ancient. With a very unusual car driving around the neighborhood. And a weirdo kid named Otto who was afraid of attics. Charley didn't want to tell his parents about any of this stuff yet. It would only get them upset.

The sky clouded for a moment. The sun fell behind a drifting cloud, throwing the house under shadow.

"That's freaky," Charley said.

"It's just late spring weather," his dad explained. The cloud passed and the sun glowed down on them again. "The weatherman predicted a chance of rain this afternoon. It'll probably just be a sun shower."

Charley still thought it was freaky the way the weather changed so quickly.

"This is what it's like living in Graves Lake Estates. This is country living, not city living. You never know what to expect out here in the country," his dad went on. "Charley, why don't you go upstairs and pick out your bedroom? Chrissy already picked out her room."

That's when it caught his dad's eye. "Look," he said, "the roof doesn't have a TV antenna on it."

Charley's dad put his hand above his eyes to block out the sun. "That really is a steep roof. I'm not sure if we can even get a TV antenna up there." He shrugged his shoulders and walked up the porch steps and disappeared into the house.

***

Soon after, Charley's mom came back outside with a tray of cold drinks. She handed the glasses around to the moving men. One of the movers said, "Sure is a hot day." He chugged down the lemonade.

"We're looking forward to this house," she said. "We used to live in an apartment back in New York."

"Well, I'm sure you'll become used to Graves Lake Estates once you live here a while," another man said. He looked different from the others. He wasn't sweaty or dirty. Charley noticed the man carried a clipboard and a cell phone.

"It's so beautiful here with the birds and the trees and the clean fresh air. We'll like it here just fine."

"Sure," the same man agreed. "It's just that sometimes

it takes city folks a while to get use to life in Graves Lake Estates. My wife and I moved out here from the city a couple of years ago. We almost didn't stay. One of our neighbors had told us a story about our house on the day we moved in. It scared my wife for a long time." The man glanced over his shoulder at the Nickels' house. "But then I guess you've heard the story about your place."

Charley's mom had an uneasy feeling. Charley could see that serious look in her eyes. "What are you talking about?"

"The locals say that the family who used to live here had to move," he said.

"Tell me what you really heard."

The man looked away. Charley could tell that the man really didn't want to tell them. "It was just a story. I don't want to frighten you the way my wife was frightened when we moved to our house in this town."

"I want to know," Charley's mom insisted.

"The family moved from this house because of some kind of creature. They said it lived in the attic."

"You don't believe that, do you?" Charley's mom asked.

"What didn't make sense was that they said the creature lived in the attic, but they insisted the creature was dead. How could something be dead and alive at the same time?" he asked.

Charley's mom stared at the man. Charley remembered what Otto had said. Maybe weird Otto had told the truth.

The man glanced at his wristwatch. "I've got another job to check up on. I've got to take off."

The man put the empty glass back on the tray.

"Thanks again for the drink," he said. "Anyway, I guess your family will find out for themselves."

It sounded strange the way the man said that, as if the man was trying to warn them about something in the house. What did he truly know, and why couldn't he tell them? Before Charley could ask him, the man was in the green Ford Bronco and driving away.

The neighbor's dog howled.

"I feel so bad for that dog," Charley's mom said.

"You shouldn't," said the other man.

"But it sounds so lonely."

"He is lonely," said the man.

"It's just a dog," Charley's mom said. "I'll have to speak to its owners one of these days. A dog should not be made to feel so lonely that it has to howl day and night."

The man did not say anything. He just looked over at the neighbor's house where the howling noise was coming from. Then he said in a quiet voice. "If you listen real good, it doesn't sound like a real dog."

"What do you mean?"

"I just never heard a dog howl like that before," the man said. "I've worked all over the country and I've heard real dogs howl but the howl that comes from your neighbor's house sounds like no howl I ever hear a dog make."

You might be right," Charley's mom said. "We always lived in the city so we don't know as much as you about dogs, especially howling dogs."

"Yeah," said the man. "Whatever is making that sound sure doesn't sound like anything I've ever heard before … except here in Graves Lake Estates."

Charley's mom and the man stared in the direction from where the howling was coming.

Charley felt it was creepy.

"Well, Charley, I think we should go find your dad now. He's up at the house by himself, and who knows what trouble he's getting himself into trying to fix the house."

A long howling sound hung in the air, and the man with whom Charley's mom was talking started packing up his tools, not saying anything more.

The howling sound grew louder, and then it was gone.

"Zombies," Charley Nickels decided. "The whole place is crawling with zombies."

CHAPTER 3

Charley's dad seemed possessed. He was opening doors and squirting oil onto the rusty hinges like a madman. The doors made ominous sounds that Charley had heard once when he was having a nightmare about dead people coming to get him—the sounds of a graveyard gate being opened and closed by rotting, walking zombie corpses!

For some reason that he didn't quite understand, this made Charley remember a time when he had awakened at dawn back in their old city apartment and walked like a ghost down the apartment stairs and out onto the silent sidewalk. There was no one about that early in the morning. There were no cars on the street. There was no life, neither people nor dogs. The early morning light had started slanting down from the sky onto the brick wall of their apartment house. He had felt odd. He had felt surrounded by brick and mortar. There was no green grass or trees or even ghost dogs howling. He had felt alone for the first time in his life. It was just the sad lonely city early in the morning, and the world seemed so empty to him that he felt like an alien. He never told anyone about that time, but that was when he first started to make believe he was a monster.

After all, everyone knew monsters weren't afraid of anything ...

The next thing Charley knew, an old woman was coming up the stairs of his new house with his mom. It was the old real estate woman who had sold them the house. He could hear her talking to his mom. He saw her mouth clattering away, like a pair of those fake spring-loaded teeth they sell in novelty stores. He remembered he saw one of those things in a novelty store once and, with its white plastic teeth and its red plastic gums, all it did was chatter, chatter, chatter. The chattering had almost driven him nuts. That's what the teeth in the old woman's mouth reminded him of. And she wore her gray-blue hair in a bun and her face was caked with too much white powder and a slash of blood red lipstick painted her mouth. Spooky, Charley thought. The real estate woman looked as if some crazy person had put her together. Charley wondered if this woman who sold them the house was ... crazy herself! Walking up the stairs, the old woman wobbled in her high heel shoes that were too big for her feet. She started to tumble backwards and his mom screamed; but just as suddenly, the strange old woman somehow managed to grab the banister to steady herself just in time.

"Why did you come back?" he heard his mom ask the old woman.

She didn't answer. Her eyes were blank, as if she wasn't even there.

"There's a story that the house is haunted," his mom said. "What do you know about that?"

The old woman made a whimpering noise but Charley couldn't hear what she was saying. Then he saw the old woman take hold of his mom's hand. The old woman was whispering and his mom's eyes widened. Then his mom turned and ran down the stairs!

Charley, standing at the top of the stairs, studied the old woman. She had blue veins in her skin. She looked like something out of a horror comic with all that bad makeup. Then she looked at Charley with those blank eyes of hers. She stared at him. Her teeth were still chattering. Her teeth were yellow. And there was this gross stuff dripping from the corner of her mouth! "You must be Charley," she hissed. "There's a door at the other end of the hall, around the corner. I just stopped by to see if it is still locked."

"What's so special about that door?" he asked.

"It leads to the attic." She said, and she didn't say anything more until she got to the bottom of the stairs when she turned around, stared a moment at Charley and told him, "Make sure that door stays locked." Charley watched her walk slowly down the stairs.

"Why does it have to stay locked," he blurted out.

But she didn't answer him.

He watched until she was almost out of the room and then she turned around and said to him, "Because it must never be opened."

A chill fell over Charley as she left the room. He felt as if he had just seen the Creep!

CHAPTER 4

Why do we wonder what possibly strange and mysterious secrets are hidden behind closed doors?

Charley stood in front of the attic door. Two small steps led up to the door, which loomed large and mysterious in front of them, as if holding guard over an entrance to another world. The door was covered with thick old black paint and had a crystal-glass door knob.

"There's something going on that I don't like," Chrissy told him. "I don't know what it is exactly, but I have this odd feeling …"

Charley asked if she'd seen the strange car outside their house earlier in the day. "It was totally weird and came from out of nowhere—breathing fire and smoke."

"Spooky."

"Way past spooky. It seemed like it was watching the

house. Like it wanted to know who was moving in."

"Maybe it used to live here. I mean, maybe the person who used to own this house was driving that car," she wondered. "I bet whoever was driving it just came by to see what the people are like who bought the house."

"That's us, Chrissy. Think about it," Charley said. "It's us that strange black car came to see."

"Sometimes your imagination really goes wild, Charley. The person driving that car just wanted see who was moving into this old house. I'm sure that's all it is."

"Except for one thing," Charley shot back. "—I don't think there was a person behind the steering wheel."

"You couldn't see anyone?"

"I mean, no one was driving the car!"

Now Chrissy wanted to get away from the attic door for sure, but Charley had made up his mind otherwise. "I'm going to open it." He stepped on the first stair.

"Leave it alone, Charley."

He stepped on the second stair. His hand was shaking. Maybe he was crazy, he thought, but he reached out for the doorknob. He reached closer ... almost there—and suddenly, just as he was about to grab it, a gust of wind blew open the window curtain and a stream of sunlight fell onto the door. The sudden sunlight struck the prismlike glass doorknob and the light exploded from the doorknob in a rainbow of reds, blues and yellows.

"Look at that," Charley whispered, amazed at what he was witnessing.

The imposing black door with its crystal doorknob that

scattered all those wonderful colors was like a frightening but beautiful sudden treasure they had found, and Charley couldn't take his eyes off it.

This was his discovery.

This was his terror.

He was told he must never open it, but a powerful need to unlock the door and find out what was on the other side seized Charley. It held him in its grip. The thought of opening the door gave him the same kind of chill as when the old woman warned him that the door must stay locked forever.

"Something tells me not to open that door," Chrissy said.

He looked at her. "I … I know what you mean"

"Let's just go, Charley! Let's get out of here."

He rolled on the heels of his sneakers, wrestling with his thoughts, struggling to make up his mind. If he turned away from that door now, there was a chance he might never want to find out what was behind it. Sometimes you just had to stop yourself from being scared.

"You go downstairs if you want," he finally told her.

"I don't think even mom or dad know about this door," she said. "It's strange the way it's hidden at the back of the house, tucked away in the corner of the hall, don't you think?"

Charley wasn't listening.

"It's the attic," he whispered, staring straight ahead. "It's the door that leads up to the attic." The door that crazy old woman had warned him to stay away from!

"Anything happens to me, you take off. Quick. You got that?"

"This is nuts, Charley."

He took a deep breath then moved to the second stair. He reached out his hand. He reached for the door. The light from the window that was reflecting off the glass doorknob got into his eyes and he had to squint to see what he was doing. Then he took another deep breath … He grabbed the doorknob—but suddenly a powerful force was hurtling him through the air, throwing him down to the floor, and Chrissy was screaming.

***

The screams echoed off the walls.

Her parents came running. "The door killed him," she shrieked.

Their dad's eyes widened with terror. He reached down and lifted Charley

"I—I" Chrissy cried, but the words choked in her throat. "Is Charley okay? Dad, tell me. How badly is Charley hurt?"

"Calm down, Chrissy," Charley's dad said, examining Charley's elbow. "It's only a scrape. Your brother's going to be all right once he catches his breath."

"So this is the door to the attic," their mom whispered, mysteriously. "This is the door the old woman was chattering about..." and in that same moment, Charley saw his dad's arm reaching for the attic door knob.

"No!" Charley shouted, his strength back.

Charley's dad turned. "What's the matter?"

"The door knob is burning hot … it must be full of electricity—"

"It's just a glass door knob, Charley."

"It's haunted. It must be. I'm sure of it—"

Charley's dad looked closer at the door knob, studying it. Then he looked over his shoulder. He pointed at the window behind him. "This glass door knob has a ring of metal around it. I bet the sun was shining in from the window and the sunlight heated up the metal part. That's why you pulled your hand away really fast—so fast that you fell!"

Charley felt like a geek.

"You need a special key to open the lock on this door," his dad said.

"What kind of special key?"

"You need a skeleton key."

"Skeleton key?" Charley tried to imagine a skeleton key. He had never seen one. All he could think of were bones and other creepy stuff. Then he remembered Otto's story—how Otto had left an ancient key in the old glass jar down in the basement just before he escaped through the window.

"Maybe we should just leave this door alone," his mom wondered aloud.

.

CHAPTER 5

Charley dug a flashlight out from his dad's toolbox. With flashlight in hand, he went over to the basement door. Charley opened the door to the basement. A cold feeling of air came up from the dark basement. Charley could see a flight of creaky wood stairs that disappeared down into the darkness. He stood at the top of those stairs, shining the light back and forth into the darkness below. He could feel the cool basement air rising ghostlike, raising tingles along his spine. The air smelled musty as it wafted around him. The basement possessed an eerie, unearthly aura; it was cluttered with all kinds of strange things. Something Charley knew from watching old monster movies was that people who lived in old houses often stored all kinds of weird things in basements. And in vampire movies, vampires always slept in basements. Basements were dark and cold so that's were vampires hid their coffins. The basement, the deep dark basement where the cool air chilled your skin, spiders spun thick huge silky cobwebs, and mice scurried across the floor. Was a coffin down in the basement? Vampires liked to sleep in their coffins full of musty-smelling soil from the mountains of Transylvania. Spiders and mice probably scampered across the dark floor but Charley couldn't see too well in the darkness. And now he even wondered if he really wanted to find that skeleton key. Maybe it wasn't so important to get into the attic to put up a TV antenna anyway. After all, Otto told him no one used antennas for their TVs anymore—people just ordered a cable connection from the cable TV company to get their TVs to work. Heck, Charley thought, it might even do him good not to watch so much TV. Chrissy told him that a lot of times. After all, he really didn't want to turn into a "Mister TV-Square-Eyes" as his sister said he would if he kept watching all those TV monster movies. Maybe there wasn't even a skeleton key, he wondered. He felt like a condemned man waiting to meet his executioner.

***

Suddenly Charley heard a sound: "Ka-*Pop!*" The basement lights flashed, then burned and lost their glow. The basement went black.

Charley jumped back. His heart skipped in his chest. Then he understood. It was just a popped fuse. That's all. There must be an electrical short in the switch, and when he flicked it on it simply blew the fuse, knocking out the lights.

Just my luck, Charley sighed. What I need right now is The Monster Fan Club here. He shook his head, thinking about Ernesto, Double-Ton, and his other buddies from the old club. "I sure do miss them," he said wistfully. "I sure do wish they were here."

Charley swayed the white ray from the flashlight back and forth across the dark depths of the basement. You're all by your lonesome and you *need* that key, that strange skeleton key, he told himself. He knew what he had to do so he took a deep breath, moving forward in this sea of darkness. His heart pounded heavier in his chest and his legs grew weak beneath him, knowing something dreadful might be waiting for him in the darkness!

"I—I can't see anything down here," Charley whispered. He swept the white ray of the flashlight in front of him. The light was like a painter's brush stroke on a pitch-black canvas. He heard a sound. He stopped and listened. Suddenly a ball rolled across the basement floor, rolled out from the darkness, rolling in front of him and then disappeared back into the darkness. Where did that ball come from, Charley wondered. The ball coming from nowhere was scary. For a moment it was hard to hear anything but the sound of his own heart pounding in his ears. "Is ... Is anyone d-down here?" The words caught in his throat. There came no answer, only the pitter-pattering sound of something, something falling. Pitter-patter. Pitter-patter-pitter ... It sounded vaguely familiar to Charley. Like rain. Then the air erupted with a roaring clap of thunder. Charley grew terrified, but the pitter-patter spraying against the basement window told him it was only a thunderclap and falling rain from outside that had frightened him.

He moved forward in the dark basement, the rain sprinkling against the glass panes. From out of nowhere, something scurried across the floor and he flung himself back. He had seen several stray cats hanging around the house earlier in the day. He tried to assure himself it was just a cat, just a stray cat ... probably trying to get out of the rain. He looked over his shoulder to make sure the door at the top of the stairs was still open. He started forward again, sweeping the flashlight back and forth, back and forth across the basement floor. He waited a moment to calm his beating heart. He tried breathing slowly—first breath in, second breath out, third breath in, fourth breath out. He had seen it done on TV and in movies. People tried to calm themselves down by regulating their breathing. As the rain stopped falling outside, he slowly breathed in, slowly breathed out ... trying to stay calm.

It seemed to take forever.

Then his eyes adjusted to the dark and he saw an old workbench. It was against the wall at the other end of the basement, and Charley aimed the shining flashlight as he groped his way toward it through the endless darkness. He could make out shapes and objects in the darkness, not much else. He realized he had forgotten how the cool, damp air enveloped him like a ghostly shroud. The air still had that sour smell to it, like the odor a wet dog gets in its fur when it comes in out of the rain. He swept the room again with the flashlight. He saw some boxes filled with old newspapers and magazines, a couple of sheet-covered chairs, an old wood chest of some sort with wide metal hinges. A small person could fit in it, he thought. But it was only a chest, he told himself. Only a chest. No way could it be a coffin. No way at all.

Then he saw it. The beam of light from his flashlight fell on an old glass jar. The light swirled in the jar, filling and overflowing it—and there was the key, the very key that would open the door to the attic! He lunged for that jar but stumbled, his legs bumping against something in the dark ... probably an old box or piece of furniture the former tenants had left behind. For some reason he raised his eyes. His eyes glanced up at the dirty, rain-streaked basement window. There was a face in the basement window. Rain-soaked hair fell over its eyes. The face stared in through the window at him. *The Creep!* He gasped, dropping the flashlight!

Shuddering with fear, he somehow grabbed the jar, but just as he wrapped his hand around it, he heard the noise again. He spun around. "Who's there?" he called into the blackness. There was no answer, only his terrified voice echoing off the cold, hard basement walls. His heart pumped like crazy. He held the glass jar and kneeled down on the grimy cement floor, searching for the flashlight. The flashlight had gone out when he dropped it, lost in the dark, but he was sure it was somewhere nearby. He felt around the grimy floor feverishly, trying to locate it when he thought he heard the noise again, a noise that this time sounded like a voice.

"Over here …"

Charley raised his head, his eyes scanning the dark. He could barely see anything, couldn't make out where the voice was coming from. His heart pounded in his chest, pounded harder than ever as he groped furiously for the flashlight, keeping his face up, trying to see who was making the sounds.

"Char… leeeeeee… I want to get back into the attic…"

It was the Creep! It was in the basement with him!

Charley's hand touched metal, and he grabbed the flashlight, flicking its switch, raising and shining its light in the direction of the voice. Then he saw it—the towering ugly green creature froze in his flashlight then slipped back into the dark! Somehow Charley scrambled to his feet. The jar in one hand, the flashlight in the other, Charley tore like a bat out of hell for the staircase. Somehow his rubbery legs moved swiftly under him. He dashed and bumped and stumbled across the dark basement, all the time trying to get to the stairs. He could see the first stair. He was almost to it. His heart pumped in his throat. The terror closed in on him. It grabbed behind him, nipping at his heels!

In a flash, Charley could see the upstairs room now. The room at the top of the stairs was bursting full of light. He was almost there, almost, just a few more—"Help me!"

Charley reached the bottom stair. He started for the next higher one. He felt a coarse bony hand grasping frantically at his ankles, almost pulling him back down into the cold, dark basement!

Charley closed his eyes. He was finally at the top of the

stairs, bent over and gulping down huge mouthfuls of fresh air. "Calm," he tried telling himself between breaths. "I— I've got to calm down ..."

***

After a while, his pounding heart slowed. He stood up and straightened his back, taking another deep breath, but this time breathing out slowly, more calmly. He was okay. Everything was okay. He noticed he was holding something in his hand, and when he looked at it he saw it was the glass jar with the ancient key in it. The key. The *skeleton key*. Then he remembered the grasping hand on the basement stairs. He quickly slammed the basement door shut behind him.

***

Charley Nickels carried the old glass jar over to the kitchen table. He slumped into a chair and stood the jar in front of him. Strands of a silky-fine spider web wavered along the inside of the jar. A fine layer of dust was settled over the key at the jar's bottom. As Charley studied the jar, he could not quite shake that feeling of terror in the dark basement. Then he looked over his shoulder at the shut basement door. He pressed his ear against the cool wood of the door, listening. He listened for the sound of the Creep behind the basement door ... it was probably still wandering around down there in the dank darkness at the bottom of the basement stairs. He listened, but he heard no one ... nothing ... not a sound. But his head hurt. It felt like a real bad headache and he rubbed his forehead. Faintly, very faintly, he heard the Creep's voice in his brain telling him to unlock the attic door!

He saw the slide-bolt on the door. The slide-bolt was thick. It looked as if it could lock out an army. The previous owners must have had a reason to install it. *Ssss-slam!*—he slid the bolt into its lock.

Just to be sure.

CHAPTER 6

"I—I don't know, Charley."

"You don't know what?"

"I don't know if I *want* to go into the attic."

"Sure you do," he told Chrissy. "Now that I have the key, we open the attic door and find out what's really up there."

"W-why?" She shivered remembering what had happened with that black attic door before.

"Why?" Charley repeated, as if the answer was so simple. "You ask me, Why?" He had a mad gleam in his eye, saying over and over, "Don't you get it, Chrissy? Don't you get it, Chrissy?"

She wanted to run. He was different—she had never seen him quite like this before. This time he was not acting as if he were a monster or an alien from another planet.

This was real. She wanted to get away from him, but she couldn't. She was caught like a fly in a spider's web. She stood frozen, as he kept asking her, "Don't you get it? Don't you get it, Chrissy? With this skeleton key I can open the door—I can get upstairs to the attic. Don't you get it, Chrissy?"

"Something is controlling your brain!" Chrissy told him.

"You think so, Chrissy? Do you *really* think so?"

She backed off.

"There's a Creep locked in the basement," he shot back. "It tried to get me when I was down there!"

"Did you tell dad or mom?"

"We can't, Chrissy. They can't know."

"But a Creep in our house!"

"I bolted the basement door real good," he said. "So it probably climbed out the basement window … We'll never ever see it again … I'm sure of it!"

Chrissy could see the orange sun lowering itself in the sky outside the hallway window. "Maybe we should come back tomorrow. This Creep thing is going to give me nightmares."

"It's now or never," he said. "Like I said, if it's still in the house, it's locked away in the basement."

He suddenly looked at her very strangely.

"Don't chicken out on me now," he told her. He walked up the two small stairs to the door and slid the skeleton key into the lock. With great anticipation, he turned the key....

Something stuck.

He turned it in the other direction.

Click.

The tumblers in the old lock rolled over in their iron casing.

Click.

They heard the bolt slide!

***

The door creaked on its rusted hinges. Charley peeked through the crack. Then Charley slowly pushed it. The old door creaked with the sound of old bones. A warm stale breath of air, like the hand of a ghost, reached out and brushed against his face. The stale ghost air rushed past him, as if escaping its jail. Charley stood in the open doorway now. He looked up and saw the inside of the attic. Heavy oak beams slanted high above him. He stood at the bottom of a dusty flight of stairs looking up at the attic that was full of shadows. Suddenly a ball rolled down the steps, bouncing as it rolled down from the top stair of the attic. As it rolled past Charley, his body tingled with fear. Where had it come from, and did someone roll it down to him? It looked just like the ball he had seen in the dark basement, and Charley was scared.

***

As Charley started up the stairs, Chrissy noticed a light switch on the wall by the bottom stair. She flicked it. A light went on in the attic somewhere. Suddenly something brushed her face. It felt like thin hair or silk, and she tore at it with her hands, trying to get it off.

Charley tried pulling it off her, but the thin strands

broke and tangled around her face.

"I think a spider got in my mouth," she cried hysterically, wiping at her mouth with the back of her hands. "What if I swallowed a spider? What then, Charley, what then?" she yelled in panic.

He grabbed her by the shoulders. Shaking her, he made her look at him. "You're okay, Chrissy. Just take it easy. You didn't swallow any spider. Just go and rinse out your mouth, okay?" He held her by the shoulder, hoping to get her to calm down. Suddenly she felt his fingers digging into her skin .... She needed to get away from him.

Somehow, she broke out of his grip.

***

Fear wrapped its paralyzing tentacles around him as he ascended the stairs into the attic of dying sunlight that filtered through an attic window and threw long shadows across the old wood. It would be dark outside soon, and the low-watt electric light was too weak to keep the dark from advancing. He climbed another step up the dusty wood stairs, now imagining a million scary images. Then he remembered his friends from back in the city. He recalled the face of each of his pals from The Monster Fan Club and he took a deep breath, raised his hand in front of his face, imagining that he was holding up a black cape. He pulled back his lips so his teeth showed. He stared straight ahead. He was like some possessed creature. "Do not be afraid of the dark," he spoke, sounding like that famous old actor in the 1930s vampire movies. "It is only the dark. The dark is my friend, for I am Drac-u-la. Count Drac-u-la.

Vampire of the night!" The stairs creaked under him with each step he took, with each stair that took him up to whatever was in the attic besides dust and cobwebs and shadows and deafening silence. He was making believe he was a monster so he wouldn't feel scared—

But he could still hear the Creep's voice ... and his head pounded!

***

In the middle of the attic, he stood looking around. It was kind of spooky, but that made it all the better. He looked up at the roof that raised to a point high above him. The attic was huge, spreading out with so much space.

The members of The Monster Fan Club would be proud of him if they knew what he had just done. He might even get them to come over to the house for a visit. And he would show them ... the *attic!*

***

Strangely, nothing was in the attic except an old TV sitting on a dilapidated table. The table had thick brass handles. Charley walked over to it. There wasn't all that much light left in the attic but he could see that the TV was a Philco. It said so right on the bottom of the TV, just above the large dials. He remembered his dad talking about owning a Philco television. His dad was just a kid back then. Charley wondered if the TV worked but suddenly he remembered that story that Otto had told him about the Creep TV, and he backed away from it—wondering if this was the same TV that Otto had told him about....

As Charley was backing away, he saw a 1950s 3-D

horror comic book sitting on the ancient table. Charley was a big horror comic book collector. He had a whole box of old horror comics. He kept each comic in its own plastic bag with a backing of cardboard so the comic wouldn't bend or crease once it was in the plastic bag. The plastic and the special cardboard protected the comics from aging. At least that's what the guy who owned the comic book shop had told him and his friends. Charley picked up the comic and blew away the dust. He would add it to his collection. Definitely. Old horror comic books were really hard to find. I really lucked out, he told himself.

Then he noticed the TV again, that old Philco. He shuddered.

There was something about that TV.

He didn't quite know, but something about it was strange. It was staring at him like an evil eye!

CHAPTER 7

Fortunately, food always made Charley feel better.

Charley's dad was carrying several festive red, white and blue buckets of Friendly Frank's Famous Fried chicken into the kitchen when Charley came downstairs. Charley's mom did a double-take. She wasn't expecting Mr. Nickels to find a Friendly Frank's Famous Fried Chicken Palace in the town of Graves Lake Estates. She had always thought that Friendly Frank's Famous Fried Chicken Palace was strictly a big-city fast-food joint. Like the one from their old neighborhood, near the subway.

"Who'd have thought Friendly Frank would have a Famous Fried Chicken Palace all the way out here," Charley's dad said.

Mrs. Nickels and Chrissy spread out the paper plates and plastic forks.

"Can we go there, dad? Can we eat at Friendly Frank's Famous Fried Chicken Palace soon? Is it just like the place in the city, you know just like our Friendly Frank's Famous Fried Chicken Palace back home?"

"We are home, Charley."

"Oh, yeah," Charley said. "But you know what I mean, dad."

"Sure I know, son. I just want you to get use to the idea that this is where we live now. It's our new home."

"Sometimes I just miss the old neighborhood," Charley said.

"I know," his dad told him. "You miss your friends and the way things used to be. But, Charley, life is full of changes and moving out here is one of the best changes our family has ever made."

"It's creepy," Charley mumbled.

"It's different, not creepy," his dad tried to explain. "I bet your new friend Otto thinks this is a pretty neat town to live in."

"I'm not sure about that. I'm not even sure if I want to be friends with Otto. Otto calls this place 'Creep Town'."

"Creep Town?"

"Creep Town," Charley said again. "He called this place Creep Town, and I don't think he was joking." He looked at his sister to make sure she didn't say anything about the creature he had seen in the basement.

The chicken tubs were steaming, wafting the smell of Friendly Frank's Fried Chicken throughout the room.

"It's going to be a long time before I let you kids eat

this greasy stuff again," their mom said.

Charley blurted out, "I'm moving into the attic—I was up there, and it's the perfect place for my bedroom. I can fix it up. There's nothing in there now except an ancient table and an old TV."

That perked his dad's ears. "What kind of a TV?"

"An old TV."

Charley could tell that his dad was becoming excited about this TV by the way his dad's eyebrows arched to form an upside down V in the middle of his forehead.

Mrs. Nickels tried to dismiss the whole issue. "Dear," she said, obviously wanting to calm her husband down, "it's probably just an old black and white TV set."

"Did you see the make? The model? Did it have a name on it?" It seemed as if a hundred questions about the TV tumbled out of his dad's mouth.

"Phil—" Charley started to say, but his dad cut him off before he could finish the sentence.

"Philco? Was it a Philco, Charley?" His dad looked so hopeful. "I used to have a Philco TV when I was your age, Charley. Oh, all the wonderful TV shows I saw on that TV. I still remember them," he added.

Charley and the rest of the family held their Friendly Frank's Famous Fried Chicken pieces in midair now. They were just staring at their dad. They were just looking at him in shock.

"Hon, are you okay?" Mrs. Nickels asked her husband.

Mr. Nickels turned glassy-eyed at her. "It's a Philco," he said, grabbing her hand. "A Philco, I bet!"

Chrissy put down her chicken wing. "Anyone want to tell me what's a Philco?"

Charley stared at his father who was sitting there in that Hawaiian shirt with a goofy happy-puppy look on his face.

"When I was a kid, my family had a Philco TV," he tried to explain again.

Mrs. Nickels just shrugged her shoulders. "Kids, your daddy had a Philco TV when he was a kid. Isn't that nice?"

"Weird," Charley whispered under his breath.

Mr. Nickels picked up a chicken leg and shook it at each of them as they sat at the table. "Now you listen here," he said, pointing the chicken leg at Charley then at Chrissy then at their mom "and you guys listen good. That TV. That Philco"—and when he said "Philco," Mr. Nickels' eyes glazed over as if he were floating in a wonderful dream— "is a special TV as far as I'm concerned. It brings back a lot of happy memories for me."

Mr. Nickels stood. "Charley, something tells me it's a good sign, finding that Philco TV in the attic." Mr. Nickels shot a look at his wife. She knew he had made up his mind. "If Charley wants to make the attic his bedroom, we'll let him make the attic his bedroom!"

This amazed Charley.

"You mean it?"

His dad shook his head. "Of course I mean it."

Then Charley looked at his mom. "Is it true?"

She thought it over a moment. "Of course, we'll have to fix it up. Clean it, paint it, put down rugs. Sure, Charley." She smiled. "If you really want to make the attic your bedroom, then we'll do it."

"And the Philco TV goes with it," his dad proclaimed.

That settled, the Nickels family returned to their dinner. It was their first evening together in the house. They sat at the kitchen table, munched on their fried chicken, and drank their glasses of cold milk. They didn't say another word to each other as they finished their meal. Except for Mr. Nickels. Every now and then he would breathe out that magical word "Philco ... Phil-co ... ooo ... oooo" and his eyes would glaze over with happy long-ago memories.

***

Could anything else weird happen?

Suddenly a bolt of lightning from outside lit up the evening sky and a crash of thunder shook the scraps and bones on their table plates. A pitter-patter of rain started falling, tap-tap-tapping against the windows, and then more lightning and thunder. Then the rain fell heavily.

From outside, on the street, came another loud noise. This was a different loud noise. It sounded like thunder, but Charley knew this time it wasn't thunder. It was a loud explosion that he had heard before. The loud noise outside on the street disrupted the Nickels family dinner. What was it? What was happening? Everyone looked around in bewilderment, but only Charley pushed away his chair. He ran over to the living room window and slid open the heavy curtains. He peered out the window. There it was. Like a bad dream. It was the old beat-up long black car—the funeral hearse—backfiring and belching smoke. It waited in the pouring rain. It waited there at the curb in front of his house. Charley shuddered, thinking it had finally come back to get him. He quickly closed the curtains and hid behind the door!

A moment later the doorbell rang.

The Thing was at the door, coming for him!

"Answer it, Charley," his mom called.

Charley couldn't tell her. The Thing at the door looked a lot like what Charley had seen in the basement window. Water was dripping down its hair, down its face. Charley was sure it had come back for him. Now it was right outside the door. Charley knew he had to be silent. Maybe, just maybe, it would go away!

The doorbell rang again.

"Charley! Don't be rude. See who's at the door!" His dad was coming toward him. Coming to open the door!

"No, dad," Charley pleaded.

As his dad turned the doorknob, Charley pleaded again, "No!"

It was too late. The door opened.

A tall, bony, mysterious figure dressed all in black stood in the doorway as another clap of thunder and a jagged bolt of lightning shattered the night. Charley froze with fear. It looked at Charley's dad, then down at Charley. A grin cracked across its face as it extended its big hairy hand out to Charley. "C. Chills Wills, TV Cable Man," it said. "Glad to meet you!"

The Thing stood half in and half outside the front door. "I'm the TV cable representative for the town of Graves Lake Estates," he said, looking at Charley's dad. Charley could see The Thing was trying to get into the house, out of the raging storm, but Charley wouldn't get out of its way.

The Thing pushed into him.

"Who are you, really!" Charley demanded.

The Thing looked back down at Charley. "Well, son," he said, "I guess you don't believe me." The Thing reached for something in his jacket pocket. "And you shouldn't believe me, I suppose," he added. "That's why I carry this." The Thing took something official-looking out of his pocket. He showed it to Charley. It was an identification badge with a blurry photograph of The Thing's face pasted on it. Below the photograph, it read "Morgue Cable Company." Below that, it read "Official Cable Representative." The signature, "C. Chills Wills," slanted across the bottom of the identification badge, written in red ink. Maybe he had signed his name in blood, Charley wondered. Charley couldn't take his eyes off it.

The Thing spoke to Charley's dad. "You must be Mr. Chambers," he said.

Before Charley's dad could answer, The Thing opened a notebook, flipped a couple of pages, and very politely said, "Oh, I'm sorry. I fear I may have made a mistake. I now see that our records indicate the Chambers family no longer lives in this house. I truly am sorry to have bothered you." The Thing turned to walk back out the door. But after he took just one step, he turned to Charley's dad and said, "Have you recently moved in? May I ask your name?"

"We're the Nickels," Charley's dad said. "This is my son, Charley." He pointed to Charley, still standing guard in the doorway. "Over there is my daughter, Chrissy." His dad pointed to Chrissy. "And this lovely lady coming into the hallway is my wife, Mrs. Nickels." Charley's dad hugged Mrs. Nickels. "And," continued Charley's dad, "I'm—"

"Let me guess," The Thing said, walking towards them. "You must be Mr. Nickels."

"The one and only," Charley's dad quipped. "That's me," he said, laughing in his Hawaiian shirt. "I'm Mr. Nickels, and these are all the other Nickels."

The Thing said, "Mr. Nickels, I'm in your neighborhood to discuss some of the cable TV channels our company is offering."

Charley's dad called to Charley. "You hear that, Charley? *Cable* TV."

"I noticed this house does not have a TV antenna on its roof," The Thing said. "And I also noticed you have a couple of charming children. I'd like to tell you about our family-oriented cable TV channels, if you could spare a minute or two."

Then Charley knew what was coming. Just as he expected, his dad pointed to Charley and Chrissy. "They are charming children, aren't they?"

"Very much so."

"Tell you what I'll do," his dad said to The Thing. "I'll trade you two Nickels for a dime."

Charley's dad was belly-laughing at this joke. Mrs. Nickels laughed too.

The Thing just stared at the family.

Goofy, Charley thought. His dad's jokes were just soooo goofy.

"Hey, kid," The Thing said. "Our TV cable company likes to give out promotional items. They are lots of fun. You want one?"

"What's a promotional item?" Charley asked.

"Stuff that promotes the company, in this case the cable TV company. The promotional items are like advertising. You know what advertising is, don't you?"

"Sure," said Charley.

"So you want one of the cable TV company's promotional items or what?"

"Okay," Charley told him.

The Thing reached into his brief case for the item. He took it out and put it in Charley's hand.

It was a ball. A ball like the one that spooked Charley in the dark basement. "I don't think I want this," said Charley.

"You don't?" said The Thing. His thick eyebrows arched. "All kids want a ball," he said. "You can play with it!"

"Not really," Charley said, handing the ball back.

The Thing returned the ball into his briefcase and just stood there staring. Then he said, "May I come into your house and sit down so we all can talk?"

CHAPTER 8

"Well, are we glad to see you!"

Charley couldn't believe his dad said that.

"Come in, come in," his dad was saying now, inviting The Thing into their house. "How about a coffee? A cold soda maybe? Sit down, sit down …"

Mr. Nickels was letting The Thing walk right in and making The Thing feel at home, too! The Thing must have hypnotized my dad, Charley thought. There was no other explanation.

Or was there?

As The Thing sat in the living room sofa, he said, "Like I mentioned before, I noticed you don't have a TV antenna on your roof."

"It's a killer roof—sharp as a tack the way it comes to a point at the top," Charley's dad said. "If I climbed up there to install an antenna, I'd slide right off the roof." Charley's dad laughed. "I'd land smack on my old big you-know-what!"

The Thing's face cracked; its lips drew back ear-to-ear in a smile. "Mr. Sharptooth, your next door neighbor, has the same problem with his roof."

Charley interrupted: "Mr. Sharptooth has a steel dog cage in his backyard. It's for his ghost dogs. I saw the cages from the upstairs window. I heard the dogs howling at the moon—"

The Thing raised his thick black eyebrows at Charley. "Ghost dogs, you say?"

Charley's dad wanted to talk about cable TV. He let the cable guy know that it would be great if he could hook up the TV set without having to climb up that steep roof to put up a TV antenna.

"Yes," The Thing agreed. "That's a good point. Mr. Sharptooth is an elderly fellow and he has been enjoying our cable TV channels precisely because he doesn't need to put an antenna on his roof. We simply run a TV cable from the telephone pole outside. We run it into your basement, then drill holes so we can run the cable upstairs to your TV sets."

"We have only one TV," Charley's dad said.

"Two," Charley corrected him. "Don't forget the TV in the attic."

"It's a Philco," Mr. Nickels boasted.

The Thing's eyes lit up. "An old Philco! Oh, you are lucky!"

That made Charley feel good. He started to think that maybe The Thing wasn't so strange after all.

Then The Thing looked at Charley with lowered eyes. "By any chance, does that Philco in the attic have a cable connected to it?"

"Yes," said Charley. "There's no roof-top TV antenna connected to it but, sure, it has a cable."

"The cable is probably for the TV antenna that should have been on the roof," Charley's dad offered.

"Very strange," said The Thing. He flipped through some papers he held in his large hairy hand. "Why, yes," said The Thing. "I see that just last year the previous owners of this house had us connect a cable to a TV in the attic."

"It must have been the Philco," Mr. Nickels said.

"Yes, but unfortunately," said The Thing, "something must have gone wrong because just a few days after we connected it those same people demanded we cancel their cable TV."

"Why?" Charley asked.

"I cannot tell you exactly why, but what happened was all very strange," The Thing told the family. "Something certainly happened, something no doubt strange, and the family who lived here before you quickly moved out."

"Why? Where did they go?" Charley asked.

"No one knows," said The Thing.

"Now that is *very* odd," Mrs. Nickels said.

"Anyway," said The Thing, "according to my records, we left the cable connected to the old TV in the attic. We had no way to get back into the house since the owners left so quickly, locking all the doors behind them when they took off."

No one said anything for a minute or two and they all sat in silence looking at each other.

"Well, anyway," The Thing suddenly said, changing the subject, "that old cable connection no longer works, so if you want cable TV hooked up to the Philco in the attic you'll just have to put in an order for a new cable TV connection."

The Thing crossed his long legs and relaxed on the Nickels' sofa. As he was talking to Charley's dad, he opened a briefcase he had been holding under his arm. From the briefcase, The Thing took out a packet of brochures. They looked like advertisements. He handed a couple of them to Charley's dad. Charley's mom brought in a tray of coffee. She started reading them, too. The brochures were colorful, shiny, with a lot of pictures and numbers on them. While Charley's parents flipped through the brochures, The Thing sipped his coffee and chatted with Charley's mom. Somebody must have said something amusing because suddenly The Thing laughed. Then Mr. and Mrs. Nickels laughed. Chrissy came over and sat on the sofa next to The Thing. And nothing weird happened. Everyone seemed to like this cable guy. Perhaps The Thing was a person, Charley began to realize. Just a normal human being. A man. That was all. Not a monster. Not *The Thing*, as Charley had thought. This guy was okay, Charley decided, even though he did drive a strange car—a strange black fire-and-smoke-belching car. He was just a salesman—a cable TV salesman. And what, besides his name—C. Chills Wills—could be spooky about that?

Then Charley noticed the guy sniffing the air, his nose twitching like a caged white mouse Charley had seen once in a science class. "I smell something delicious," C. Chills Wills announced.

C. Chills Wills jumped up from the sofa. "Friendly Frank's Famous Fried Chicken?" he asked, a shining in his eye. "Am I right?"

"We were just eating in the kitchen …" Charley's mom was saying, when C. Chills Wills said, "May I?" C. Chills Wills was pointing to the kitchen.

"You want to go into the kitchen?" Charley's mom asked. She looked at Mr. Nickels, puzzled, and shrugged her shoulders.

"I'd love to," said C. Chills Wills, and he was already halfway across the living room floor. "Maybe I'll have just a bite," he said, as he disappeared into the kitchen.

The Nickels family all looked at each other. C. Chills Wills was tall and gaunt, his skin pale as whitewash paint. He surely did look hungry, Charley thought. There was no question about that. Still, wasn't it kind of odd the way his nose caught the smell of the leftovers and the way he wanted to go into the kitchen like that?

Well, maybe his parents didn't think it was all that strange, but Charley surely did.

While the Nickel family waited in the living room, Charley walked over to the kitchen door. He could hear something. Crunching sounds. He pushed open the door a crack. He peeked into the kitchen.

C. Chills Wills must have heard Charley. He spun around. "Oh my dear boy, please do come in and join me," C. Chills Wills said between crunches. Pieces of chewed stuff came dribbling out of his mouth.

For a moment Charley couldn't move because he couldn't believe what he was seeing. C. Chills Wills held a paper plate full of chicken bones. And C. Chills Wills was eating the chicken bones!

C. Chills Wills eyes glowed as he crunched the bones in his mouth. "I just love Friendly Frank's Famous Fried Chicken bones … don't you?"

All Charley could do was shake his head.

Then all of a sudden C. Chills Wills swallowed the mouthful of bones. Charley saw C. Chills Wills stretch his neck to get the bones all the way down when he swallowed.

"Burp," said C. Chills Wills after he swallowed. He patted his hand on his chest. "Oh dear, but do excuse me. I ate so fast, I hope I don't get indigestion."

C. Chills Wills put down the empty paper plate.

"Now I must return to the living room so I may tell your family all about the wonderful world of Morgue Cable TV." With that said and done, C. Chills Wills swept right past Charley, strode across the living room floor, plopped back down into the sofa, and sipped from a cup of coffee.

Charley didn't move for what seemed to him a long time. He just stood there in the kitchen doorway, his brain trying to make sense out of what his eyes had just seen.

***

Back in the living room, they all made small talk for a while about the many channels cable TV provided its viewers when the cable guy—this Mr. C. Chills Wills—put down his coffee cup and said, "Yes, that's a good point, Mrs. Nickels. As a matter of fact, I think you and your family will better understand the cable TV channels I'm selling as I tell you more about them." Charley saw C. Chills Wills's eyes scanning the living room as he talked. What was he looking for, Charley wondered. Maybe he wasn't just a regular human after all. "By the way," C. Chills Wills continued, "I see you have a new stereo system. Are you interested in music?"

"We love music," Charley's mom answered. "I especially love classical music."

"Then I'm sure you'd be interested in subscribing to our special music channel. It's called 'The Classical Channel'."

"How much?" Charley's dad wanted to know. "How much does it cost?"

C. Chills Wills picked up his coffee and took a leisurely sip. "Before we discuss money, Mr. Nickels, I'd like to ask you a question or two."

"Shoot," Charley's dad said.

"In fact," C. Chills Wills said, "I'd like to find out a few things about your interests and life-style. Morgue Cable Company offers many TV channels, and I want you to buy the ones you will like best and will use most."

Charley couldn't help it, but a rush of words burst from

his mouth as he blurted out, "You've got a cable TV channel for monster movies? I like monster movies. Scary monster movies."

A very weird look came over C. Chills Wills's face when Charley said that, and he stared at him.

"Quiet, Charley," his dad said.

"Your son has quite an interest in monsters I can see," said C. Chills Wills. He was still staring at Charley and Charley was starting to feel uncomfortable. "Do monsters scare you, Charley?" C. Chills Wills asked. "Or do you, Charley Nickels, scare monsters?"

Yipes, thought Charley—this guy is out of his mind!

Finally, C. Chills Wills looked away from him and asked his parents about the kinds of TV shows they liked.

In the meantime, Charley wandered over to the window. He wanted to see that strange car again. As he slowly pulled back the curtain so he could look out the window, he heard C. Chills Wills probing his parents with such questions as:

"What shows do you like to watch on TV?"

"What movies do you like to watch?"

"Tell me more about your interest in Hawaiian shirts, Mr. Nickels."

"Chrissy, do you like cartoons?"

"Do any of you have special hobbies? Do you watch a lot of sports? Have you ever seen the science fiction movie channel, U.F.O? Are you familiar with the sports channel, S.W.E.A.T? …"

Charley stopped listening. He was too busy looking at

that long black car parked outside in front of his house. He wondered if there was a coffin in the back of the car. He jumped—a bolt of lightning flashed across the night-sky. The lightning bolt almost hit the black car. As the flash momentarily lit up the night-sky, Charley noticed the huge shiny chrome grill on the front of the car. The chrome grill was full of many pointed rows of metal, sharp as sharks' teeth. It looked hungry, as if it needed to be fed, Charley thought, shivering as he saw that.

The sound of the conversation changed, and Charley turned around to listen.

"I see," said Charley's dad. "It makes a lot of sense."

"I certainly understand," his mom added.

The way his parents were talking now, it seemed that they were under the spell of C. Chills Wills.

"That's a good point."

"That's true …"

C. Chills Wills had somehow hypnotized them— Charley was sure of it now, as his father chanted over and over, "I want cable TV. I want cable TV …"

C. Chills Wills took a pen from his shirt pocket. Charley saw him click it. C. Chills Wills put the pen in Mr. Nickels' hand. Then he put a contract agreement on the coffee table. He pushed it in front of Charley's dad. "Just sign on the dotted line, Mr. Nickels," C. Chills Wills was saying. A loud thunderclap exploded outside in the storm. And like a zombie, Charley's dad did just what C. Chills Wills asked— he signed the contract!

***

After Charley's dad signed the contract, C. Chills Wills neatly folded the contract and quickly slid it into his briefcase. Then he gingerly brushed something off his jacket sleeve. Another flash of lighting ripped the night, hurtling shadows across the living room.

***

Charley's father ended up ordering the sports channel, his mother got the gardening channel, his sister chose the cartoon channel, and when it came his turn, Charley asked again if there were any channels that showed monster movies.

C. Chills Wills didn't answer Charley. He only gave him that weird look like before.

"It's been a pleasure doing business with you all," C. Chills Wills said to the Nickels family. "Is Thursday or Friday better for us to install your cable TV? Do you want both TVs hooked up or just this one in the living room?"

"Hold on," Charley said. "You didn't answer my question."

C. Chills Wills growled: "We've got a science fiction channel, we've got a fantasy channel, or how 'bout the travel channel?"

Charley said no to all of them. As C. Chills Wills was packing up his brochures, folding away his order form and getting up to leave, he suddenly snapped his fingers, looked Charley in the eyes and said, "Listen, kid, I'm not supposed to sell this yet. You see, it's just being tested now … but maybe I can break the rule for you, kid, seeing how much you like the creepy, crawly, spine-tingly stuff." But then C.

Chills Wills stopped, thought about it a little, shook his head and said, "No. No, perhaps it's better I don't tell you about it."

"Why not," Charley said.

"I really shouldn't even mention it," C. Chills Wills said.

"You can't do that. You have to tell me."

"No I don't" said C. Chills Wills. "I don't have to do anything."

Charley persisted. He hounded the cable guy to tell him. And only Chrissy noticed it wasn't like Charley to act so obnoxiously. She wondered if it was possible that the Creep was back—trying to control Charley's brain again!

"Kid, I suggest that you watch your daddy's sports channel, or your sister's cartoon channel, or even your mama's gardening channel," C. Chills Wills told him. Then he leaned over and whispered in Charley's ear: "This is just between you and me, kid, but those creeping begonia flowers on the gardening channel give me the cold willies!"

Charley pulled away—the cable guy's breath stunk like the garbage pail in his school cafeteria.

"Anyway, kid," C. Chills Wills continued, "your family already ordered enough cable TV channels to keep your head spinning for months. You don't need another TV channel."

But as the salesman was about to walk out the front door, he stopped, spun around, flashed his crazy smile and said, "It's called The Monster Channel, kid," as he handed Charley his *private phone number* business card, "and you'd be the first kid in the neighborhood to have it, if you want it, and if your dear old dad and mom allow you to order it."

Another lightning bolt flashed as C. Chills Wills opened the door to leave.

Charley watched him walk through the pouring rain to the long, black car that sat at the curb, waiting. And thunderclaps filled the night until C. Chills Wills's car was finally out of sight.

CHAPTER 9

Charley couldn't wait for the cable TV connection. He kept thinking about all the different TV channels he would soon be able to watch. But what he really wanted was The Monster Channel. All weekend he pleaded with his parents to get him The Monster Channel.

"It's not fair," Charley whined one day. "Everybody got to pick a cable channel except me."

"You wanted The Monster Channel, but Mr. C. Chills Wills said he couldn't sell it yet," Charley's dad reminded him. The family was outside, hanging out in the backyard. Charley's mom was weeding her flower garden and his dad was watering the lawn. Chrissy was just sitting in the shade, sipping an iced tea.

"Mr. C. Chills Wills told you that he wasn't allowed to sell anyone The Monster Channel. The cable TV company must test it before they can sell it," said Charley's mom.

"But you don't understand," pleaded Charley, "I must have The Monster Channel. I need The Monster Channel. And I want it. *Now!*"

Charley's parents stared at him like he was from another planet or universe. He was all bugged out, and when Charley Nickels bugged out, it wasn't a pretty sight.

"He's going to turn into Frankenstein," his sister warned them. "I know that look on Charley's face. Other kids hold their breaths until they turn blue, but Charley might turn into Frankenstein or Dracula. He might even turn into the Wolfman, and then he'll start howling."

Finally Charley's parents told him that if he really wanted it, he would have to act like an adult and call Mr. C. Chills Wills himself.

Charley spun around and jumped onto the porch. As he ran into the house, he remembered the cable TV guy's business card. The card had the salesman's private phone number printed on it.

He decided to call immediately.

***

Charley Nickels didn't waste a minute. He picked up the telephone in the kitchen and dialed the number on the card. Everything would be cool, he told himself. He would definitely be the first kid on the block to have The Monster Channel. But as he called on the phone, he thought about that creep cable TV guy, C. Chills Wills. The same C. Chills Wills he had seen in the kitchen eating those Friendly Frank Fried Chicken bones! Charley almost gagged just thinking about it. Then he heard C. Chills Wills's telephone ringing on the other end of the line, and Charley Nickels got a major dose of the cold willies when he heard C. Chills Wills's voice.

"Yeah," said the voice, "what do you want?"

Charley was perspiring. He stuttered, "T-This is Ch-Charley N-Nickels."

The voice boomed back. "Who?"

"Charley Nickels. You signed up my parents for some cable TV channels over the weekend."

The phone went silent at the other end. At least, in the sense that Charley couldn't hear the voice. But there were other sounds. Strange sounds. Charley listened, trying to make out the noises.

"Oh, sure," the voice suddenly came back. "Now I remember. The new family."

"We just moved into the neighborhood, that's right," said Charley.

"So what do you want? You better not be calling to cancel our cable TV deal."

"No," Charley said, "that's not what I'm calling about."

"It's not?"

"No," said Charley. "In fact, we can't wait for our cable TV."

"So you're complaining that it's not hooked up yet, is that it?"

"That's not why I'm calling."

"So what do you want?"

"I want The Monster Channel," said Charley. "I want

the special cable for it connected to my TV in the attic."

"The Monster Channel?" the voice said. Suddenly Charley heard the voice roaring with laughter on the other end of the phone. It sounded like a maniac laughing!

"This is the kid," said the voice. "Am I right?"

"Charley's my name."

"The kid wants The Monster Channel," the voice said again, and the voice laughed like a maniac again.

"Is this C. Chills Wills?" Charley anxiously asked.

"The one and only."

"I thought so," said Charley, imagining the creepy TV cable guy. Charley got another shivering case of the cold willies, but there was no way he was going to hang up the phone until he got his TV channel.

"I told you The Monster Channel is not ready yet," said C. Chills Wills. "Quit annoying me, kid."

Charley waited, his ear to the phone. He heard those strange sounds in the background. He didn't hear C. Chills Wills. But he did hear something. He wasn't sure what it was.

Charley waited.

And waited.

"Okay, kid," said C. Chills Wills. "If you're going to be such a pest, then I guess I have no choice but to give you The Monster Channel. I'll send one of the cable installers over first thing—"

"And remember to tell them to connect The Monster Channel to the TV in my bedroom," Charley excitedly blurted out. "My bedroom is in the attic—the same place as my TV."

"Oh, it's your TV now," said C. Chills Wills. "Did the old owners give it to you?"

"Don't make a joke," said Charley. "You know when my family bought the house the old owners didn't want the TV. So it's mine now."

"Sure, kid," said C. Chills Wills. "The cable installer will make sure *your* old TV in your bedroom gets a special cable connection to The Monster Channel. Okay?"

"Okay," said Charley.

"One more thing I must tell you, kid," said C. Chills Wills.

"What's that?"

"Just don't blame me if something terrible happens to you while watching The Monster Channel! Like I said before, kid, The Monster Channel is a new cable channel. It has never been really tested. Anything can happen!"

C. Chills Wills roared with the laughter of a madman.

Charley slammed down the telephone.

CHAPTER 10

On Monday, Charley and Chrissy woke early to catch the school bus. Charley didn't care too much about school. He could take it or leave it. He was the new kid on the block, which meant he was the new kid in school. And that wasn't the greatest thing in the world. Luckily, he knew that monsters were always like the new kid on the block. For example, Charley knew that in the movies Dracula and Frankenstein were always different from everyone else because they stood out like sore thumbs. Charley had seen so many of these monster movies that he knew being the new kid on the block, odd-man-out, wasn't so bad. Charley knew that was because Dracula and Frankenstein were different, special—creatures with powers greater than the typical person. In a way that was cool, Charley had long ago decided. He didn't ever want to be like everyone else. He liked being like Dracula and Frankenstein. They were special. That's why they were cool.

***

Those first few days and nights in the new neighborhood came and went without much of anything special happening. While the workers were getting the attic ready for him to move into, Charley slept in the bedroom across the hall from Chrissy. He didn't even set up the place where he slept in Chrissy's room. He just left all his stuff in the boxes that the moving men had left scattered around the room. The only things he unpacked were some clothes for school and the olive wool blanket for sleeping in the big bed.

Every afternoon when Charley got back home from school, he watched the big sweaty workers trudging up the attic stairs. He watched the workers place plywood over the attic beams. Then they hammered nails into the plywood. It was all hammering and heavy footsteps, filling the house with all manner of sounds. The racket was music to Charley's ears. He couldn't wait to move up to his attic bedroom.

By Thursday of that week, the workers finished. Before they left, they helped Charley and his dad lug a bed, a dresser, and a big old rug up the attic steps. Charley and his dad unrolled the rug after the workers left. Later, while Charley unpacked his boxes of stuff, his dad fiddled around with the old TV—the Philco.

"Do you think it still works?"

His dad removed the back of the TV. "There's some

kind of strange stuff in there," Charley's dad said as he poked around the inside of the old television. "Stuff I never saw inside a TV before."

That's where it lives, Charley thought, but instead of telling his dad that the strange stuff might belong to the Creep, Charley's dad was busy screwing the back of the TV in place. "I tightened a couple of loose wires," his dad said. "Let's try it out."

Charley's dad picked up the electrical cord and plugged it into the wall outlet. His dad turned the big dials and suddenly the old TV's empty black screen filled with a white light as the electricity flowed through it.

"It's alive!" His dad hissed, feverishly adjusting knobs and dials. "Alive!"

Charley came over for a closer look. He saw his dad's face bathed in the white glow of the lit TV screen. His dad looked like Doctor Frankenstein in the movie when the crazy doctor brought the monster to life in the old lab during the lightning storm.

Charley jumped back.

His dad turned away from the TV and looked at him. His dad had a weird gleam in his eye.

The TV screen flickered behind his dad but there was no picture. Only white light filled the TV screen. The glow washed over his dad.

"Wow—it still works!" his dad exclaimed.

"Almost, you mean. There's no picture."

"Picture? Picture? Don't worry about it not having a picture yet!"

Charley had never seen his dad so excited before. His dad even looked happier than the time he bought his Hawaiian shirt.

It was a little spooky to see his dad acting this way.

His dad turned off the TV. "It needs an antenna to get a picture."

"We can hook it up to the cable," Charley suggested.

"You mean *when* we get the cable," Charley's dad mumbled. "C. Chills Wills promised the cable company would send some guy over to install it, but we've been waiting three days and no one has shown up."

Charley and his dad sat together on the rug in front of the old Philco.

"Do you think we'll ever get our cable TV hooked up?" Charley asked.

His dad snapped his fingers. "Darn right," he said, with a sudden renewed enthusiasm. "I want to see the old Philco full of TV life, and the only way that's going to happen is if I go downstairs right now and call Mr. C. Chills Wills, pronto. The Nickels family is going to get its cable TV."

Charley continued unpacking his boxes and setting up his attic bedroom but as he unpacked his comics, he glanced over at the Philco TV. For a moment, he wondered why his dad thought that old TV was so special. After all, it was just an old TV—a big square box of old electronic stuff and wires. Yeah, he told himself, just an old junk TV.

Or was it?

CHAPTER 11

Charley got a good night's sleep. The headaches had disappeared and he felt like his good old self again.

"Charley," his sister asked at the kitchen table that morning, "you weren't scared?"

"Scared of what?" He gulped down his glass of orange juice.

"Of sleeping in the attic. I think the attic is a spooky place. I keep thinking about the Creep."

Charley leaned back in his chair and crossed his arms. "Fear is nothing but what's in your head," he said. "If you think something is scary, you'll get scared."

"But what about the Creep?"

"That must have been something I made up in my imagination," he answered. "I've seen too many monster movies, I guess."

Their mom came over to the table. "You both better finish your breakfast. The school bus will be coming in a few minutes."

Charley grabbed a slice of toast.

Just then, their dad padded into the kitchen. He was still wearing his bathrobe and slippers. He was all scruffy and unshaven.

"The only thing we have to fear is fear itself," their dad said, stretching and yawning. He was half awake; his eyelids looked heavy. He plopped down in the kitchen chair. "Coffee?" he asked.

"It's already poured. It's in the cup in front of you," Mrs. Nickels told him.

Charley's dad stared down at the cup of coffee, looking at it as if he was waiting for the cup of coffee to float up off the table and pour itself into his mouth.

"Your dad's a real sleepy head," their mom said. "He was up all last night watching TV."

"The only thing we have to fear is fear itself," he said again.

Charley and Chrissy just stared at their dad. He was really starting to act weird, more and more, Charley decided.

Charley thought: That's what happens to parents when they get older: They weird out. The only thing more weird, Charley decided, was if his dad had slept in his favorite Hawaiian shirt. That really would have been too weird a sight for breakfast.

"What do you mean, dad?" Chrissy asked.

Mr. Nickels was sipping coffee. Charley could see that his dad was waking.

"It's a famous quotation."

"What's a quotation?" Chrissy asked.

"When you say or write something using the same words someone else said or wrote. That's called a quotation. For example, the former President of the United States, Franklin D. Roosevelt is famous for saying, 'The only thing we have to fear is fear itself.' I said it exactly as he said it, word for word, so it's a quotation."

Mr. Nickels took another sip of the coffee.

He put the cup back down on the table.

"You see, kids," he explained, "Franklin D. Roosevelt said those words in a speech to the people of this country when he was inducted into the Presidency. Times were difficult, scary, and he wanted to make the people feel less fearful. He said that way back in the 1930s."

Charley stared at his dad. "Why was everyone scared," Charley asked. "Did they have the Creep back then, running around and scaring them?"

Mr. Nickels looked at Charley. "You know, son," he said. "What you told Chrissy is the same thing Franklin D. Roosevelt was trying to tell the people of this country and the world."

"I still don't get it," Chrissy said. "What does it mean?"

Mr. Nickels picked up his coffee. "It means exactly what Charley said earlier. Basically, Charley and Franklin D. both were saying that there is nothing really frightening in this world, except for what we put in our heads. Ipso facto," Mr. Nickels continued, "there is nothing to fear except the idea of being afraid."

"Hey," their mom called, "look at the clock. You kids better get going or you'll miss the school bus."

They pushed their chairs away from the table as their mom handed them their books and lunch bags. "Have a good day," she wished them, pecking them each a kiss.

"Bye dad," Chrissy said.

"Bye kids," their dad answered.

As they opened the door to leave, Charley turned around. He didn't know exactly what it was, but he felt there was something strange and he asked, "How come you're just waking up, dad? You usually would have gone to work by now."

Their parents turned and stared at the kids. There was that same strange look in their dad's eyes as when he was up in the attic trying to get the old TV to work.

Their mom began to fidget. She looked nervous, but finally she was able to say, "You're dad was up very late last night. He hardly slept."

"But why?" Charley had to know.

Mr. Nickels put the coffee cup down, but as he started to answer, their mom said, "I don't think you should tell them yet."

"Tell us what?" Charley asked.

"What is it we shouldn't know yet?" Chrissy asked, too.

"We'll talk later," their mom told them. "I don't want you kids to miss the school bus."

"But mom," Charley pleaded.

"Go to school, kids. Go to school now," their mom said. "There's the bus."

The yellow school bus was pulling up to the curb in front of their house. There was something definitely strange going on, Charley wanted to shout, but he realized instead that he and Chrissy were running across the front lawn now, running to the waiting school bus.

"The only thing we have to fear is fear itself," Charley told himself when he got into the bus.

CHAPTER 12

"Did you see that look on dad's face?" Charley asked Chrissy for about the fourth time that morning. They were on the school bus, sitting across the aisle from each other. Each time Charley asked his sister that question, he had to shout so she could hear him. Some of the other kids were looking at him as if he were a space case, but Charley didn't care what the other kids might have been thinking about him right now. "It was just like that time dad found my new Nebulous Buster video game that I installed on his computer," Charley continued. "Don't you remember, Chrissy? Dad kept playing that game over and over. He got so much into that computer game it that he stayed up all night playing it. Mom finally had to pull the plug out of the computer to get dad to stop."

"Dad did get a little nuts back then," Chrissy agreed.

"Now don't you get it, Chrissy?" Charley yelled. "He had the same nuts look on his face this morning. I bet he didn't even go to bed last night!"

"But you took Nebulous Blaster off dad's computer," Chrissy reminded Charley.

"That's what I mean, Chrissy—this time something else is making dad act weird!"

"Dad's just stressed out," said Chrissy.

"What about me?" said Charley. "This town is full of freaks, zombies, and weirdos of all kinds. I'm really stressed out!"

"That barking dog doesn't let me get a good night's sleep," added Chrissy.

"Mom seems ok," Charley said.

"Because mom keeps herself busy most of the time," said Chrissy.

"Yeah, but have you seen how she has been acting lately? I'm kind of worried about both of them," Charley added.

"Hey," Chrissy told Charley, "you're acting the weirdest of all if you want to know the truth."

Charley said nothing. He knew his sister was right.

***

The bus was finally pulling up to their school when Charley's sister told him, "I don't think it's anything to be concerned about. Like I keep telling you, I think dad was just sleepy."

"Sure," said Charley, as he was getting off the school bus, behind his sister. "The question is … Why didn't dad sleep last night? I mean, dad's usually asleep the moment his head touches the pillow."

"Charley, you're letting your imagination get the better of you again. Next thing you know, you'll be telling me that some kind of crazy creature kept dad awake."

She means the Creep, Charley thought. He kept thinking about that. It was really odd. Almost impossible. At breakfast that morning Charley had decided there were no such things as real creatures or monsters. Maybe his dad just couldn't sleep last night. No reason. Sometimes people just can't sleep. It all made a lot of sense when he thought about it like that.

"But what if …?" Charley started to say under his breath. "What if something more is going on and no one can explain it? What do you do when no one can explain the unexplainable?"

CHAPTER 13

The old TV roared alive! ALIVE! There in his attic bedroom, Charley's dad was sitting at the foot of the bed staring at the old TV. The whole room was dark except for the white glow that the TV screen cast over his dad's face. And his dad just sat there with a crazy look on his face. Charley heard more screams and splattering noises. The screams grew louder and shrill and suddenly his dad was throwing his head back in spasms of loud maniacal laughter! "Dad! Dad!" Charley yelled, but his dad kept rocking back and forth at the foot of Charley's bed, possessed by the glowering TV—Charley thought his dad must be watching a monster movie but then he saw that there was no picture on the TV ... The TV screen was filled only with bright white light washing over that insane look on his dad's face! Charley yelled again, "Dad!" This time his dad slowly turned his head. He stared at Charley. His dad was staring at Charley as if Charley were that old TV set! "Dad!" Charley shouted again, but this time he shouted out of fear. His dad's eyebrow arched like upside-down Vs and his mouth drew back from ear to ear so that his dad looked like a real madman! Terror paralyzed Charley, but somehow he managed to scream—screaming and screaming until his throat closed ... he was choking! He felt his throat closing, getting tighter and tighter ... he couldn't breathe! He gasped one final time for a breath of air but the choking grew tighter and tighter, and then he realized that two powerfully strong hands were clasped around his throat, choking him! "No, dad," he tried to say, "don't do it!" But suddenly the hands around his neck were not the hands of his dad—the hands belonged to the Creep! The Creep's ugly face leaned over Charley, stuff dripped from the Creep's mouth, and its hands gripped tighter and tighter around Charley's throat!—And all of a sudden Charley bolted up, throwing the covers off of him, gasping for air ... air ... air!

Finally he woke. His heart was pounding, but he was able to breathe.

***

"I had a terrifying nightmare last night," Charley whispered to his sister as they sat at the kitchen table, doing their homework.

Of course Charley didn't have to tell her that. She felt concerned about her brother's irrational behavior ever since he had found that skeleton key that opened the door to the attic.

"Yeah, Charley. I'm not surprised."

It was getting late. There was school tomorrow. They had eaten supper, and now they were sitting at the kitchen table trying to finish their homework. Suddenly Charley dropped his pencil.

Chrissy looked up from her notebook. "What is it this time, Charley?"

Charley stared at her, frightened. "What if I have another nightmare tonight?"

"I don't think it was a good idea for you to move into the attic. It's making you act creepy," she told him.

"Yeah, maybe," Charley said, picking up his pencil, "but what if it happens again? What if I see dad sitting in front of that creepy old TV in the middle of the night?"

Chrissy shook her head. She couldn't believe he was talking about it again. "I don't want to hear anymore," she told him, closing her school book. "I don't want to hear one more word about it."

***

Their mom came into the kitchen. She had a big smile on her face. "I've got a surprise for you, kids." She told them that the man from the cable TV company came over and connected the cable to all the TVs in the house.

"That's great," said Chrissy. "I guess they connected the TV today when Charley and I were in school. Right?"

Their mom didn't answer immediately. After a few moments she said, "Well, not really."

"What do you mean?" Chrissy asked. "We didn't have cable TV before today."

"Your father and I didn't want you kids to know, but the cable man came over *last* night to hook up the TV."

"Last night!"

"We were afraid you kids would stay up all night watching the new cable TV if you had known."

Charley blurted out again, "The cable TV was working last night, and no one knew?"

"Like I told you," their mom said, "I knew about it."

"And dad knew," Charley guessed. "Am I right?"

"You're dad stayed up all night watching cable TV," their mom said. "I wasn't very happy about that. And he missed work today," she added

Charley and Chrissy looked at each other in amazement. Maybe Charley's dream had not been a dream after all. Maybe, just maybe, Charley did see their dad in front of the old TV set up in the attic late last night!

"By the way, Charley," his mom said, "Mr. C. Chills Wills telephoned today. He said to tell you The Monster Channel is hooked up on your TV set. He said he did it special for you."

"The old TV in the attic?" Chrissy asked.

"That's right," their mom said.

"Mom?" Chrissy started to say.

Charley knew what his sister was going to ask next.

"Was dad watching cable TV in Charley's room last night?" Chrissy wanted to know.

Another bizarre gaze fell over their mom's face. "I-I don't know," she answered, her voice sounding weird and frightened. "I thought your dad was watching TV downstairs in the living room last night."

Chrissy grew more concerned. "All night? Are you sure dad didn't go up to Charley's bedroom in the attic to watch TV?"

"I-I don't know," their mom stammered. "I'd rather

not talk about it, kids. All I know is that I was sleeping while your dad was up all last night again, watching TV someplace in the house."

Charley had heard enough. He went into the living room. He wanted to see if his dad was watching the TV there. When he got into the room, the TV was off.

Charley headed back to the kitchen. As he got to the staircase, he happened to look up. His dad stood at the top stair, looking down at Charley. He was wearing the same rumpled bathrobe and clothes that he had been wearing earlier that morning when Charley and Chrissy had gone off to school. His dad needed a shave. His hair was a mess. He yawned, and then he smiled at Charley.

"Are you going to bed?" Charley asked.

"I'm just waking up," his dad said.

"Waking up?" Charley asked, amazed. "But it's night, not morning," he told his dad. "People sleep at night, not during the day!"

"Vampires sleep during the day. You should know that, Charley."

Vampires! Was his dad telling him something? Was his dad turning into a vampire, maybe?

"Well," said his dad from the top of the stairs, "it seems that from now on I'm going to sleep during the day instead of during the night."

Charley couldn't believe what was happening. His dad used to always sleep at night. His dad used to always be the first one to get up in the morning, cleanly shaved, showered, and dressed in a fresh shirt, tie and jacket for work.

"But you have to get up in the morning to go to work," Charley said.

"I think I'll watch TV instead of go to work," his dad said. "TV is more fun than work."

"I don't get it," Charley told him. "What's going on? Why do you have to stay up all night watching TV?"

From the top of the stairs, Charley's dad just winked at him. He scratched his head and yawned. "You want to know why I want to stay up all night, Charley?"

Charley wanted to dash back into the kitchen to get his sister and his mom, but his legs wouldn't move. He stood there alone with his dad looking down at him from the top of the stairs.

"Well, it's simple, Charley. It's because all the good monster movies are on TV late at night. That's why, son. Do you find that strange?" Then Charley's dad took something out of his pocket. He began bouncing it where he stood at the top of the stairs. It looked like the same ball that had rolled out of the darkness and across the basement floor!

"Where did you get that?" Charley asked.

"What?" said Charley's dad.

"That ball," Charley wanted to shout.

"This ball," Charley's dad said. "I don't know. I don't know where I got it."

Charley just looked at his dad. He didn't know what to say. His dad was acting more and more like a zombie, and it spooked Charley. Then Charley wondered if something had taken control of his dad. Maybe Otto was right, he thought. Maybe those stories about the house and the weird TV in the attic bedroom were true. Could it really be true, he wondered. Was the Creep in their house ... taking over his family?

CHAPTER 14

If the Creep was in the house, Charley knew he would have to find it before it turned his family into total zombies! That's how creatures and monsters did it in the movies and the comic books. There was no other choice. Charley was sure of it. There was only one thing to do, and that was to get the Creep before the Creep got him!

Charley turned away from the staircase and took off for the kitchen. Charley called, "Dad's coming down and he's acting real strange."

"He just didn't get any sleep last night," she said. "After he drinks his coffee, your dad will be his old self again."

"I hope so," Charley said. His mom was cooking up a plateful of eggs for his dad. "Who eats eggs at night?" Charley asked.

"Your dad does—now!" she said without looking at

him. "I know it seems strange, but this is your dad's breakfast."

"But he should be eating supper."

"This whole house is becoming turned around," she admitted. "I hope tomorrow your dad decides to get up in the morning like most people. His boss called again. The boss wants to know why your father didn't go to work."

Charley's mom put the plate of scrambled eggs on the kitchen table.

"I don't want your father to lose his job because he can't wake up in time for work," She added, pouring the black hot coffee into their father's favorite cup.

"Do you want some breakfast, Charley?"

He studied his mom. She seemed as if she were going nuts too. "Mom, I just finished supper. Don't you remember?"

"Oh, I forgot for a moment," she said.

Charley worried about his mom now. The only one the Creep still hadn't got to was Chrissy, it seemed. He had to find her right away and tell her what was happening.

"Where's Chrissy?" he asked.

"Watching TV," his mom said.

"Oh, no," Charley gasped. He spun on his heels and almost stumbled into his dad. He scrambled away, out of the kitchen. In the hall, he heard the TV. He followed the noise into the living room, where his sister was sitting on the couch watching TV.

"Chrissy," he called, "I think something has happened to mom and dad!" But his sister didn't look at him. She was staring into the TV. She was staring into the TV and she didn't even hear him!

He was too late, he decided. He stood there in the doorway looking at his sister. He felt as if a cold wind blew over him. He watched her helplessly, and he shuddered in fear. The Creep's got her, too, Charley told himself; the Creep has taken control of Chrissy and his parents.

Charley tore out of the room, as fast as his legs would carry him.

There was no one to help him now. He not only had to save his parents, but he had to save Chrissy, too. Who knew what the Creep would end up doing with them? And he had to do it all by himself because he was the only one the TV Creep had not gotten yet. In fact, Charley was sure that he was the only one left in his family who still had his own brain!

He ran up the stairs to his bedroom, telling himself that he was the only one who could save his family!

***

Charley threw himself on his bed. He kind of wanted to cry, but he knew crying never solved anything. Sure, it made you feel good sometimes to let all your fears and problems flow away in a river of tears, but only by taking action against your fears and problems could you solve them. That was something his parents had taught him, and he knew it was true. He told himself to be brave. He knew more about creatures and monsters than probably anyone else. He had read all those comic books and seen all those movies about monsters. And he was a member of The

Monster Fan Club, wasn't he? He sure did wish The Monster Fan Club buddies were around now. But this time he was on his own. He was alone in a new town with new people. He would just have to find a way to defeat the Creep himself. He still had his brain, at least.

"I am Uno, Master of One," he reassured himself. "I am the master of my own fate. So come on genius," he added. *"Think!"*

***

Charley racked his brain for the answer. He pulled himself away from the bed. He walked across the bedroom. He had an idea. I think I know what I have to do, he told himself. The TV was still sitting on the ancient table, just as he had found it when he first went up to the attic. It seemed to be watching him. It followed him around the room. It was like a ghostly eye. He walked closer to it.

Charley Nickels turned on the TV. Light flashed from the TV screen ... And there it was, just as promised—The Monster Channel!

CHAPTER 15

In the glow of the light thrown by the old TV, Charley Nickels pulled out his comic book collection. He dug out that 1950 3-D horror comic he found when he first moved into the house. Bloody corpses and drooling creatures screamed out at him from the comic book's gory cover. He opened the comic to the first page. A pair of 3-D cardboard glasses fell out of the comic. He picked up the glasses. He glanced at the TV. Of all things, The Monster Channel was showing a weird movie called *Return of The Creep*.

Charley looked at the horror comic he held in his hand. He read the advertisement for the glasses. It read, "Put on these 3-D eye-poppers and run for your life as monsters come alive!"

Maybe this was the answer. Maybe these glasses were the key, Charley thought. If he could make the Creep in the ancient TV appear, then maybe he could capture it! He was sure that if he could capture the Creep, he could get his family back to the way they were before!

Charley slipped on the glasses. He faced the TV. He squinted his eyes. As the film credits rolled, the TV screen filled with gory, blood-dripping words. The bloody words splattered across the TV screen. A terrified woman, her hands raised across her eyes, began shrieking. The dark ominous shadow of a towering, menacing creature hovered over her!

"It's Back—And Worse Than Ever ...

It Slobbers!

It Slimes!

Don't Walk—

RUN!

From The Return of *The CREEP!*"

yelled a blood-curdling voice from the TV. The frightened-to-death woman screamed and screamed and screamed. Charley wanted to tear off the 3-D glasses, but he could not move. The TV held him, trapped. Suddenly a small round ball fell out of the TV and rolled towards Charley. Charley stared as the strange ball rolled to him. And then the horror sprung to life! The creature—the Creep—leapt from the eerie TV. It was alive! It was real! The Creep stretched to its full height there in Charley's bedroom. Lake weeds hung from the Creep, and the Creep stunk like dead fish. Drippy thick green slime drooled from the Creep's mouth. The Creep reared back its ugly green head. It opened its mouth of yellow teeth. The Creep bellowed out a maniacal laugh.

The insane sound roared through Charley's brain and Charley shook with fear.

"W-what are you?" Charley cried. "Get away from me!"

The Creep glared at Charley. "Beware the Creep, kid!" it screamed back at him.

"Stay where you are! Don't come near me!" said Charley.

The Creep lurched at Charley, and Charley ran into the corner of his room. He felt as if he was going to pass out from the terror. His heart raced, it hammered in his chest!

Slime slithered out the side of the Creep's rotted mouth. "I'm your worst nightmare! You cannot kill me because I am already dead!"

Charley tried to scream for help but the words were afraid to leave his mouth.

"And I've come to take you back with me to the watery grave where I drowned with my family in Graves Lake many years ago."

The room began spinning. Charley's heart felt like it was about to burst through his chest. The fear overwhelmed him and he found himself stuttering, screaming back at the big green Creep, "Th-this is crazy!"

The Creep roared that maniacal laughed again.

"This is insane!" Charley shouted. "You're mad, I tell you! You're crazy!"

Anger boiled in the Creep's eyes, and the Creep spun around, seething. The big ugly green thing tore through the attic, destroying Charley's room, pulling the drawers out of Charley's dresser, grabbing Charley's clothes and throwing them all over. The demented Creep dumped Charley's box of comics onto the floor. It truly was mad! It really was insane! What kind of creature had the old TV unleashed upon the world! The raving Creep ran back and forth across the attic room, round and round in circles, a monstrous tornado from another world!

Charley's mom yelled from downstairs. She called up for Charley to turn down the racket. She thought the noise was coming from Charley's old TV. The Creep hypnotized Charley. Charley wanted to run, to escape, but he could not move. The Creep was pulling stuff out of the closet now. The Creep scattered all of Charley's jackets, sneakers, and jeans.

Charley's dad knocked on the attic door. "Are you okay up there?" The Creep froze. Charley's dad opened the door a crack. The Creep didn't move. It didn't make a sound. Charley tried to answer, but it was as if a giant skeletal hand had risen from the grave and wrapped its powerful skeleton fingers around his chest, catching the words in his throat.

"You sure you are okay, Charley?"

Charley somehow grabbed a deep breath. "Sure," he uttered. "I'm fine."

"Then go to bed, Charley. Turn off that noisy TV."

The Creep shot a dead-man's look at Charley. Charley could barely stand the sight of the horrific creature! The Creep's red, bloodshot eyes burned across the room at him. The Creep's voice howled in Charley's brain. It howled, *I'm not ready to go back in the TV. I like it better out here!*

Charley's dad banged on the door again. "Are you sure

you're okay, Charley?"

"I'm all right." Charley wanted his dad to go away. He was afraid the Creep would do something terrible if his dad came into the room. "Whatever you do, please don't come up those stairs—don't come up to the attic," Charley whispered.

"Sleep well, Charley."

"Sure," Charley called down the attic stairs. He heard his dad's footsteps fading.

***

Charley's brain reeled in terror, his body perspired, his legs shook—trapped in a room with six feet of ugly, slimy, green Creep blocking the door!

But somehow Charley found the courage to shout, "I know you did something weird to my family—you put them under your spell!"

Foul-smelling vapors shot from the Creep's mouth, and it grabbed a glass of water off Charley's night table and gripped it in its green slimy hand—the Creep's maniacal laughter echoing in Charley's brain again and again until Charley's head pounded in pain! The Creep snorted, laughing like a madman, grabbed its head with its left hand, lifted his head off its body, and then with its right hand, the Creep poured the glass of water down into the hollow stump of its neck!

Now a voice came out of the Creep's head. It was the voice of Charley's dad coming from the Creep's mouth! "Go to bed, Charley," the voice said.

"What did you do to my dad!" Charley cried out with

horror.

"I bet he'll love it here," the voice of his mom said out of the Creep's mouth.

"Leave my mom alone!" Charley demanded.

Another voice came out of the Creep's head. "I don't think it was a good idea for you to move into the attic. It's making you act creepy." It was Chrissy's voice!

Charley pressed his hands over his ears. It did no good. The Creep was talking through Charley's brain and no one else in the whole world could hear the Creep!

"I nearly squashed you, honey. I could have run you over as easily as if you were a little toady!"

Whose voice was that, Charley wondered. He had never heard that voice before! "Wh-what do you want from me?"

The Creep put its head back on its body. It stared at Charley through those red, bloodshot eyes as the green slimy stuff continued dripping from its mouth. "Don't mess with me, kid," the Creep hissed, "or I'll get you next—I catch kids who go into attics alone, especially if they watch too much TV! Attics are so dry and warm, and watching too much TV is boring—wouldn't you rather be drowned in the weeds of a watery grave at the bottom of a deep, dark, cold lake?"

Charley had seen enough! He ripped off the 3-D glasses and turned away from the TV. Suddenly, the TV sound went silent and there was no picture on The Monster Channel. Charley, without the glasses, walked over to the hissing, fuzzy TV screen. "Whoa, that was too weird," he said, turning off the TV.

The TV's eerie glow faded slowly as Charley put the 3-D glasses back inside the old horror comic book. With the TV's eerie glow fading away, darkness filled the bedroom.

***

In the dark room, Charley heard a bone-chilling cry. He went over to his attic bedroom window and looked out.

The neighbor's ghost dog was howling. Charley stood in front of the attic window, looking out to see what was out there. He saw the moon, shining large in the night outside. The ghost dog howled again, and this time Charley dove into bed. His heart thumped in his chest as he pulled the covers over his head, too afraid to get out of bed to run downstairs.

CHAPTER 16

Exhausted, Charley Nickels fell asleep. His head still hurt, but as he drifted off into unconsciousness he realized he had never seen anything like the Creep, not even in his comic books. When he used to hang out in the old neighborhood at The Monster Fan Club, he and his friends discussed all the different kinds of creatures they knew about. Of course, there was Frankenstein, Dracula, the Wolfman, the psycho with the hockey mask, the madman with razor-blade-fingers who terrorized kids in their dreams. But no one except weird Otto had ever known about the creature called the Creep. Before Charley fell off asleep, he racked his brain wondering why almost no one else had heard of the Creep.

Suddenly Charley opened his eyes, remembering the cell phone that Otto had given him in case something like this happened. The cell phone was on the night table. Charley grabbed it. Back under the covers, he turned on the cell phone. Would Otto be awake at this hour? Charley dialed Otto's phone number several times, trying to get Otto to answer. There was a lot of static, and then he heard Otto.

"I saw it," Charley called into the cell phone. "You were right!"

"You must pull out the TV cable," Otto told him. "Pull out the cable or the Creep will escape again. Pull it out to be safe!"

"Too late," Charley called back. "The Creep is out of the TV and I don't know where it is."

"What do you mean?" Otto said.

"I saw the Creep when I put on these weird 3-D eyeglasses I found in an old horror comic book. I was watching the old TV when the Creep appeared. Strange, but as soon as I took off those special glasses, the Creep was gone!"

"Did you pull out the TV cable like I told you?"

"No," Charley answered. "I *told* you it was too late."

"You should have pulled out the old cable like I told you that day you first moved into the house. And, Charley, you should never have hooked up that new cable to the TV! Now I don't know what's going to happen."

A blast of static filled the airwaves and Otto's voice faded. Charley tried getting Otto back on the cell phone, but there was no answer.

As Charley turned and tossed, remembering that gruesome scene of the creature removing its head, Charley's mind and body somehow gave way to sleep …

Charley Nickels was hoping to awake from a nightmare. Instead, he awoke into a nightmare …

***

In the dark haunt of deep night, the moon hung like a lynched corpse. Sirens screamed, piercing the neighborhood silence. Charley sat up in bed, gasping for breath. This was not his imagination.

Rubbing the Sandman's dream-dust from his eyes, Charley looked toward the window. Wind rattled the glass panes. Bright white lights suddenly cut open the night. The white lights, high above the trees, swept the sky. The lights searched back and forth over the street, the trees, and the houses.

Charley pulled the covers over his head. He pressed the pillow over his ears and shut his eyes as tight as he could.

***

The next morning, Charley woke in a cold sweat. The bedroom was wrecked. All his shirts and shoes were thrown crazily in piles on the floor. His jeans were draped over the lamp. There was no doubt anymore. This was proof that the Creep had been in his room last night!

Now Charley knew for sure that if he were to catch the Creep, he'd have to do it here in the attic. After all, here was the old TV, and the old TV was the Creep's resting place. Sooner or later, the Creep would return to the TV. And Charley would be waiting. He was determined to catch the Creep and free Charley's family.

Downstairs, in the kitchen, Charley and Chrissy ate

breakfast.

"What do you think all that noise was last night?" Chrissy asked. "It was so spooky. I even saw lights in the sky."

"Don't even ask," Charley warned her. "It's all part of something you don't want to know about."

"Sometimes the police use helicopters," their mom said. "Those were police sirens you heard and police helicopter lights you saw."

"No …" Charley didn't finish the sentence. He couldn't tell his mom about the Creep. If he did, she might not believe him. Or worse, she might believe him. And if she believed him—then what?

As Chrissy and Charley were walking out of their yard to wait for the school bus, they saw a policeman. He was looking around in front of Charley's house.

"I guess you kids heard about the break-in at the hospital last night," the policeman said. "We gave a good chase, but he lost us near here someplace." The cop mumbled while he poked around in the bushes, looking for clues.

"What did he look like?"

"Big ugly fella," said the cop.

"Green, maybe?" Charley asked.

The cop stopped poking around the bushes. "You mean like the color green?"

"Yeah," said Charley.

The cop scratched his head. "Did you see something kid?"

"I think so."

"Something big, ugly, and green?"

"Yeah," said Charley.

The cop doubled over laughing. He didn't believe Charley. Charley couldn't blame the cop. Who could believe the Creep was real? No one. Except for that weird kid, Otto.

The cop continued to laugh. Suddenly a small ball rolled out from under one of the bushes. The ball stopped at the cop's feet. "Hmm," the cop said. "What's this ball doing here?"

Charley was sure the ball came from the Creep. "Kick it away," Charley warned the cop.

"It's just a ball," said the cop.

"No," Charley shouted. "Don't touch it!"

The cop laughed, reaching down for the ball. As his hand started to grab it, the ball turned into a green snake. The snake hissed and the cop jumped back, trying to pull out his gun but the snake quickly slithered back into the bushes and disappeared.

"If I hadn't seen that with my own eyes I would never have believed what had just happened," the cop said, wiping the fear of perspiration from his frightened face. Finally, he caught his breath long enough to say, "I don't know what exactly is going on, kid, but I'm getting out of here."

***

As Charley walked on to the bus stop, he wondered if the Creep could have escaped into town last night. Maybe the

Creep robbed the hospital. Anything was possible. Maybe it had something to do with those 3-D glasses, the sirens, the lights in the night sky, those hideous screams when he telephoned that strange C. Chills Wills?

Halfway to the bus stop, Charley decided that the Creep may have sneaked back. The Creep would need a place to hide. Perhaps the Creep sneaked back to the attic to hide in the old TV. Charley dashed back into the house. But in the front hall, he grew too scared to go upstairs to his attic bedroom. As he stood, terrified, in the front hall, he heard the school bus. Mr. Tate, the regular school bus driver, was hitting the horn, waiting for him.

"Go without me," Charley pleaded in a low voice. Of course, the driver could not hear him. Charley wanted the driver to go away so he could hunt for the Creep. Even though the Creep scared him, he felt he had to find the creature.

The driver hit the horn again.

"Don't wait for me. I can't leave the house," Charley said in the empty hallway.

The driver hit the horn a third and forth time.

Charley wanted the bus to leave.

"Just go away," Charley kept whispering.

But the bus driver would not stop hitting the horn.

Another cold shiver ran down Charley's back. He remembered how the Creep had warned Charley not to mess with him, and Charley ran for the bus.

It was the safest thing he could do.

CHAPTER 17

Too many strange things were happening!

Charley sat in the front of the school bus as it bounced along the road. Kids were yelling and laughing. Charley was waving his arms, trying to describe to Otto how the Creep had escaped.

"Your sister, the Earth Lady, sure is quiet," Otto said.

"I think the Creep's turning her into a zombie!"

"A zombie?"

"A TV zombie," Charley said. "The Creep has her under a spell. It happened when she was watching TV. I'm sure that's how the Creep gets people under its power."

Otto forgot Charley's sister. He realized the Creep could be a serious problem. He looked Charley in the eye. "I knew it was trouble when you called me on the cell phone," Otto said. "That's why I gave it to you when you moved into that house. I knew there was something terrible in the attic."

Charley agreed. "I should have listened to you. I just didn't believe it at first …"

The next thing they knew, the driver swerved the bus, narrowly missing a little girl, and all the kids screamed. It was a close call. Too close. The driver slammed on the brakes. The bus skidded to a halt.

The driver opened the bus door.

As the scared child got on the school bus, Charley, who was sitting behind the driver, swore he heard the driver hiss, "I nearly squashed you, honey. I could have run you over as easily as if you were a little toady!"

Charley couldn't believe the bus driver's words. Those were the same words, spoken in the same voice the Creep had said last night in the attic.

The bus pulled up to the school. He saw something even more mind-boggling. He saw a spittle of green slime dripping from the side of the bus drivers' mouth—green dripping slime just like the Creep's!

"Otto," Charley cried, "let's get out of here quick." They pushed their way off the bus and broke into a run.

"Did you see it?" Charley asked after they ran into the school. "Did you see it?"

They gasped for air in the hallway. Otto and Charley looked out the school window as the bus driver drove out of the parking lot.

"I saw it," said Otto. "I sure did!"

***

Everyone in class was talking about the sirens and skylights from last night. Some kids said the sirens and lights were an invasion of aliens from another planet. Other kids said it was a police chase. Charley and Otto just sat there. All of a sudden, Charley spoke out. "It's the Creep. I let the Creep out of the TV!"

If his regular teacher Mr. Nitpick had been there, Charley would have asked him about the Creep. But Mr. Nitpick wasn't in school today. Instead, they had a substitute teacher.

When Charley told everyone about the Creep, the kids wouldn't believe him. Only Otto believed Charley. Even Mr. Elias, the substitute teacher, felt Charley was making up a story.

Mr. Elias' favorite subject was plant science. "Besides being a teacher," he said, "I am a botanist. That's what they call someone who studies plants."

Mr. Elias just wanted to talk plants, plants, plants. Mr. Elias had brought a whole bunch of plants from his home to show the kids. The plants were all over Mr. Elias' desk. He showed the class his favorite plant.

"This plant is special," Mr. Elias said. "It's called a Venus flytrap." He pulled a glass jar out of his briefcase. The jar was full of live insects. "Watch this," he said.

Mr. Elias opened the jar. He reached in and grabbed a bug.

An odd look glazed over Mr. Elias's face as he brought the bug near the plant. The plant's leaves sprung open. The leaves opened wide like hungry mouths. Mr. Elias dropped the bug into the plant. The leaves snapped shut. The plant was eating the bug!

The class gasped in amazement and terror.

Charley tore out of the science room and dashed down the hall, wondering if the visiting science teacher was the Creep in disguise—hiding out in the school, maybe waiting to feast on a student the same way he fed the bug to the plant.

As Charley ran down the hall, the school bell rang and school was over. Otto caught up with Charley just outside the building.

"We better walk home," Otto said. "I don't think we can trust the bus driver."

"I think Mr. Elias is really the Creep," Charley told him. "I think the Creep took over his body the way he took over the bus driver's body."

"This is weird stuff," said Otto.

"Do you think it's possible?" Charley asked.

"Sure," said Otto. "Anything is possible."

***

When they got to Otto's house, Charley said, "I have to find a way to capture the Creep."

"My dad has all kinds of electronic gizmos," Otto suggested. "I bet we can catch the Creep with them." He agreed to bring over a whole bunch of his dad's electronic stuff to Charley's house after supper. "Electronics are tricky," Otto cautioned, pushing his thick glasses up the bridge of his nose. "Anything can happen. You know the voice in the car that tells you to buckle up your seat belt? It once said my name. I mean, it *knew* my name. We're living in a very weird world."

Charley and Otto stood outside Otto's house, hatching plans to capture the Creep. Finally they agreed that the only way to get rid of the Creep was to capture it on something called a Holographic Recorder, and press the Erase button. There was just one problem: What if the Creep got Charley and Otto first?

***

Charley's parents were out when Charley got home. He looked around, but the house was empty. Or at least, he thought it was empty.

Charley heard sounds coming from the back of the house. He went to investigate. Looking out the window, he saw an odd figure shoveling dirt in the backyard. Charley was sure the stranger was ... digging a grave. Then all of a sudden the stranger dropped the shovel and walked to the house. Charley heard the back door squeak on its rusty hinges. Charley hid in the corner of the room and watched the stranger walk into the kitchen. Whoever—or whatever—it was, it appeared old, wrinkled. Was that the Creep? Silently, Charley watched as the stranger stood at the kitchen sink. He had his back to Charley. All Charley could see was the wrinkled hand turning the water faucet, filling a glass with water. The water fizzed. The stranger moved his hand to his face. The stranger moved closer to the sink, and Charley saw the wrinkled face reflected in the mirror hanging above the sink. Charley couldn't believe what he saw next: The stranger was taking out his mouth.

The stranger put it into the glass!

Now Charley was sure that the Creep could assume many disguises—Mr. Elias, the substitute teacher ... the bus driver ... and now this!

CHAPTER 18

Charley opened the refrigerator. He was scared, but he was hungry. He needed a snack. As he looked for something to eat in the refrigerator, Charley noticed a plastic bag containing a soggy red thing dripping on the refrigerator shelf. "Gross," Charley gasped. He wondered if it was a human organ—maybe a human liver—that the Creep had stolen from the hospital. And in the sink was the glass of water with a mouthful of teeth in it!

Charley grabbed the phone, steadying his hand long enough to dial Otto's house. The phone was busy. He ran upstairs to his bedroom, and grabbed the cell phone. "Bring your stuff up to my room quick, Otto," he shouted into the cell phone. "The Creep is in the house!"

***

When Charley's parents got home, Charley told them the police had been looking for a monster that escaped from his TV last night.

"I think you should move out of the attic," his mom said. "That place gives you nightmares."

"The attic is not the problem," said Charley. "It's that TV. I don't want it hooked up to The Monster Channel anymore."

"I like the attic now," said Chrissy.

Charley turned around when he heard her say that. He stared at her. He couldn't believe she said that because she had always been afraid of the attic.

"You're afraid of the attic," Charley told her.

She seemed to be looking through him. "Now I like the attic," she hissed. "And the old TV, too ..."

Charley stepped back. He thought he saw green slime at the corner of her mouth.

"But you begged us for The Monster Channel," his dad said.

Charley spun around. "I made a mistake," he said to his dad. "I really don't want The Monster Channel anymore."

Green slime dripped from his dad's mouth. "You're a big boy, now Charley. You'll have to call the cable TV company yourself to disconnect The Monster Channel."

It was impossible, Charley thought wildly! He had to warn his mom. He had to tell her that Chrissy and his dad were turning into Creeps. He ran into the kitchen to tell her, but when she turned around, he saw more green slime!

The whole family was turning into creeps!

Charley grabbed the telephone. There was no time to lose. He dialed the cable TV company. But to make matters even weirder, when Charley tried to cancel The Monster Channel, the telephone operator at the cable company told him that no one had ever heard of The Monster Channel!

"What do you mean? It's on my TV," Charley insisted. "And it's making my whole family nuts!"

"I'm sorry, sir," said the lady at the TV cable company, "but we do not offer The Monster Channel as a cable channel. You must have the wrong number."

"I have to speak with Mr. C. Chills Wills!" Charley cried into the phone.

The cable TV operator asked, "Who is this?"

"Just tell him it's Charley. Charley Nickels!"

She hung up the phone.

Click.

The telephone went dead.

***

Charley saw Otto coming across the front lawn. Otto was lugging a bunch of electronic gizmos. Charley ran outside to help him.

"Quick," Charley said, grabbing the portable computer and another strange technology gizmo, something Otto told Charley was a Holographic Recording Technology machine that Otto's dad had brought back from some far-away country. "We've got to get this stuff up to my attic bedroom before my parents see us. The Creep is in the house. He even put a plastic bag with some bloody thing in our refrigerator—I think it was a human liver—I *saw* it!"

"How far has it gone?" Otto asked.

"I'm sure the Creep has my family under its spell!"

Otto gasped.

"They've got green stuff coming out of their mouths," Charley exclaimed. "Just like the Creep."

From out of nowhere came a loud explosion. The smoke-belching black hearse pulled up to the Nickels's house. C. Chills Wills stuck his head out the car window. "The cable TV station called me on my cell phone. I heard you were having problems with The Monster Channel," C. Chills Wills said. "I was afraid of that. Should never have told you about that channel. But don't worry," he added. "I've taken care of the problem." He pulled his head back into the weird car and drove off.

Charley and Otto watched the black hearse disappear into the night.

CHAPTER 19

Charley and Otto raced upstairs to Charley's bedroom. There was only one way to know if C. Chills Wills was true to his word, and that was to see if The Monster Channel was still hooked up to Charley's old TV.

"Not yet," Otto yelled.

"I almost forgot!" said Charley.

Otto put the Holographic Recording Technology machine on a table. "It's called a Holographic Recorder—that's the short name for the machine," Otto said quickly. "We have to hook the Holographic Recorder up to the computer. Quick. Before the Creep finds us here."

"Gotcha," said Charley. He grabbed the computer cable from Otto.

"Plug your end of the cable into the socket in the computer," Otto instructed.

"Which socket? The computer has several sockets!"

"The socket with nine pins," said Otto. "It's the small round one, the only socket with nine pins."

Charley found the right socket. He plugged in the cable. "The computer is hooked up to the Holographic Recorder," he told Otto. "Now what?"

Otto scrambled over to the old TV. "I'm going to hook this end of the cable from the computer to the TV. You have a screw driver?"

Charley remembered the screw driver his dad left behind when his dad was trying to fix the TV a few days ago. "Under the TV," Charley said. "See it?"

"I see it," Otto called. He grabbed the screwdriver. He attached the connectors to the cable.

"Done!" Otto called.

"Now what? Is that it, Otto?"

"One more thing," Otto said. He ran over to the bed where he had left the camcorder. "I have to connect the camcorder to the Holographic Recorder." Otto grabbed the camcorder and ran over to the Holographic Recorder. "There's a socket plug here somewhere," he said, looking for the connector hole in the back of the Holographic Recorder. "But I don't see it."

Charley panicked. "What do you mean, you don't see it? I thought you knew all about this stuff."

"It's a new holographic recording technology. My dad just brought it back from one of his trips to the Far East. I never played around with this model before."

"Well this is no time for playing," Charley yelled. "The

Creep could burst in here any moment."

"I'm trying, Charley!"

"The Creep could be in this room even right now—hiding in the closet or under the bed!"

Otto punched his fist into the air. "Shazam!" he shouted. "Done. It's all hooked up." He grinned at Charley. "I hooked up the system—we're all set to catch the Creep!"

***

They turned off all the lights in the room. The attic was pitch dark now. Otto, standing at the portable computer, pressed the On key. The computer screen lit up. A glowing gyroscope revolved slowly in the middle of the computer screen. The light from the computer reflected in the boys' faces.

"Now what?" Charley whispered.

"From this computer, I can control all the electrical equipment. Watch." Otto typed something into the computer. Charley heard the Holographic Recorder start. Otto typed something else.

"Now stand here at the computer keyboard," Otto told him.

"Where are you going?"

"I'll be right here, don't worry," said Otto.

"But what are you going to do?"

"Some one has to hold the camcorder," Otto explained. "When the Creep comes in, I'm going to record him through the camcorder. The camcorder is hooked up to the Holographic Recorder and the computer. As soon as I have the Creep in the camcorder lens, I'm going to yell, 'Now!'"

"Then what?" Charley asked.

"Then you press the Enter key on the computer," said Otto. "The computer will transfer the image of the Creep from the camcorder lens into the Holographic Recorder—we'll have the Creep trapped in the Holographic Recorder. As soon as the Creep is in the Holographic Recorder, we'll press the Erase button and delete the Creep from the universe!"

"You really think it's going to work?" Charley asked.

"We'll find out soon enough," said Otto. "Remember you once told me that you're Uno, Master of One?"

Charley's face glowed in front of the computer. "Sure," he said.

"Then, my friend, Uno, you must have faith that we will succeed. After all, only one person can be the master of your fate. And that person is you."

Suddenly, Charley realized that Otto wasn't so weird. He realized that Otto was his friend. A friend he could count on.

"From now on, I'm not going to call you Otto," Charley told him. "From now on you are going to be known as Doctor O."

Otto smiled from across the room. "Thanks," he said.

"No problem," said Charley, as he looked around the dark attic. "I just have one more thing to say."

"What's that?" his friend asked.

"I just hope we make it out of here alive …"

CHAPTER 20

They waited.

They stood in the dark room with all the electronic gizmos humming away. If they could only wait long enough, and quietly enough, it was possible the Creep would fall into their trap.

For a while, nothing happened. Maybe the Creep was too smart to fall into their trap. It was possible the Creep knew what the boys had planned. He might not show up. He might not even be in the house anymore. But the boys waited. And waited. It seemed to take forever …

Then it came suddenly.

"You cannot destroy me!" It was the Creep. From somewhere in the dark attic the Creep bellowed, "I am the power. No one can stop me now that I have escaped from the TV!"

Charley shouted into the darkness. "You release my parents and sister or Doctor O and I will wipe you off the face of the Earth!"

The room rumbled. Charley and Otto grabbed the table so they wouldn't fall. The house shook to its rafters; the air in the attic grew cold and damp. The smell of decay filled the air, and suddenly the Creep took shape in front of the boys' very eyes.

The Creep's face formed into a hideous sneer. He bellowed his maniacal laugh. "Charley! Charley!" he shouted, "I told you that you and your friend Otto cannot kill me—I am dead! Dead! And you cannot kill the dead!"

Though terrified, Charley shouted, "Release my family! I demand that you leave them alone!"

"I, the dead of Graves Lake Estates, hold dominance among all!" the Creep shouted. "On the very day that you and your family moved into this house, you became mine! Mine! Do you hear me, Charley Nickels? Your family, and soon you, shall be mine!"

Charley grabbed a chair. He started swinging it at the Creep. "Leave us alone," Charley yelled.

In the fury of Charley's wild chair swinging, the Creep changed form. It became invisible.

"Where did that monster go?" Charley yelled.

"Into energy," Otto said. "The Creep is a monster energy field. It can take any shape or form it wants. That must be it, Charley—"

"You mean it's a ghost?"

"Something like that," Otto guessed. "An energy

capable of taking any form it wants. B-But—"

"—But what, Doctor O?"

"Whatever it is, it is pure evil!"

***

For a while it seemed the Creep had gone. The room grew quiet again. The cold clammy air grew warmer. The smell of death that had permeated the room seemed to be fading.

"You think it's gone, Doctor O?"

"No ... It's waiting. It's waiting for us to make a mistake. Whatever you do, Charley, don't leave the computer."

Suddenly the Creep's voice boomed out of the Holographic Recorder. The voice boomed out in a wild maniacal cry, growing louder and louder! Somehow the camcorder had caught the Creep in its lens and photographed the monster, trapping its energy field in the Holographic Recorder.

"Now, Doctor O!" Charley shouted, realizing what was happening. "Hit the Holographic Recorder button. Erase the Creep now—"

"No!" the Creep shouted.

Otto hesitated.

"If you try to destroy me, you'll destroy your family!" yelled the Creep.

Otto shot a look at Charley. "Do you believe that?"

Fists pounded on the attic door. It was Charley's family. His parents and Chrissy were screaming from outside to unlock the door. Charley cried, "Don't come up here—don't open the door to the attic!"

But it was too late.

They broke the door off its hinges. Charley peered over the attic banister. His family stood at the bottom of the attic stairs.

"It's a trick!" Charley screamed to Otto. "We have the Creep trapped. The Creep is in our power. Do it, Doctor O—do it now!"

"Your family is mine!" the Creep roared. "Destroy me and you destroy all you have in the world!"

"He's lying, Doctor O!" Charley screamed. "Do it now. Bleep the Creep!"

Otto punched his fist into the air. "Here goes!"

"Erase him," Charley yelled. "Nuke the Creep!"

Otto slammed the Erase button on the Holographic Recorder. The computer, the TV, and all the other electronic gizmos in the attic bedroom flashed, sparks flying everywhere.

"N-n-nooo!" the Creep screamed from somewhere deep inside the Holographic Recorder. It was a gut-wrenching, stomach-churning scream of sickening pain and blood-chilling terror. In the same moment, Charley looked over the attic banister and saw his family shattering like glass statues at the bottom of the attic stairs! Charley closed his eyes, and he and Otto pressed their hands over their ears. The room seized in a vicious storm of electrical charges, swirling in lightning and thunder! And then, several moments later, it was over. The room was silent. The computer screen flickered and came back on …

Otto ran over to the attic stairs. "Your f-family … T-they're all gone …"

"That … wasn't my family," Charley cried, hoarsely. "It was an illusion created by the Creep in order to save itself."

"H-how do you know?"

"I left the door open when you and I came up here. I knew the attic door wasn't locked … so I realized the Creep had created an illusion when it looked like my family broke down the door!"

***

It was over.

Charley and Otto were still shaking with fear, but it was over. The TV horror nightmare was gone. It was over.

Or was it?

CHAPTER 21

Charley turned on the old TV. He was no longer afraid of that old TV now that he and Otto erased the Creep in the Holographic Recorder.

Bright, white light glowed out of the TV.

"I am alive!" a voice screamed from the TV.

The boys froze.

"Doctor O!" Charley shouted. "We didn't destroy the Creep!"

Otto frantically searched the Holographic Recorder. "How? How did it survive?" he cried to know.

"Do something!" Charley yelled, desperately.

The Creep howled. "I am coming back to get you boys!" Suddenly its voice changed. It was using Charley's voice! It said, "Are you trying to tell me that something dead lives in that house?"

Charley ran over to Otto. "I goofed," Otto yelled. "I hit the Play key on the Holographic Recorder by mistake!"

The Creep called out of the TV in Otto's voice, "In the attic—that's where I saw it. You see, the attic door was locked but there was this kind of ancient key in the lock. So I opened it. I went up there. It seemed strange. The place smelled like old tombstones in a cemetery at night just after a rain storm ... I know things, you see. I mean, I know what a cemetery smells like at night because I once went to a cemetery at night with my cousin, Benny. Benny's got a car, you know."

"The Creep has become us," Charley yelled. "It's speaking our words, in our voices. That's the same stuff we said when we first met each other!"

"TV is my life," the Creep said in Charley's voice, repeating something Charley had once told Otto.

"Char ... leeeeeee ....," the Creep snarled in its own creepy bellowing voice. "You watch waaay too much TV!"

Charley stumbled back. "You were supposed to hit the Erase button, Doctor O," he cried.

"I know," Otto shouted. He kept hitting different keys on the computer, desperately trying to make something happen.

Charley pleaded, "What are we going to do now, Doctor O!"

The TV fizzled, crackled, a monster movie scene appeared, then a puff of smoke; and the boys heard the television sounds—sounds of actors' voices and movie music—fading away. Suddenly, there was the Creep's face on the TV screen again. It seemed to be screaming to get out, and the boys stood terrified. Then C. Chills Wills's voice came out of the old TV set, saying:

"We interrupt The Monster Channel to let our audience know we have been informed that the Creep continues to stare at you from your TV screen. Don't be alarmed. Our chief engineer assures us that this strange phenomenon is the result of an electronic explosion in our broadcasting studio that burned the Creep's image onto the inside of your TV screen. The image of the Creep will fade out in a few hours."

It was gone. This time the Creep was truly gone.

"I can probably fix your attic TV sooner if you want," Otto offered, teasing Charley now that he realized the Creep was just a burnt image on the old TV screen.

"Don't even think about fixing that old, creep TV," Charley said. "I'm still not convinced the Creep is gone forever."

"But they said so on TV, Charley. No wonder C. Chills Wills didn't want to sell you the Monster Channel. He was right—the channel wasn't tested yet."

Charley shook his head. He wasn't totally sure of anything right now. But he knew what he was going to do. And he went over to the TV and pulled out the cable.

"You can never be too sure," he said, throwing the cable into the corner.

CHAPTER 22

The attic stairs creaked with ghostly footsteps. Charley and Otto heard the footsteps coming closer to the door.

Fear gripped them both.

Slowly the bedroom door opened.

There, in the doorway, stood Charley's mom. She held two trays of steaming food. It was a great relief. The Charley and Leo, exhausted, devoured the food.

"Charley," his mom asked, "did you meet our retired next door neighbor? He spent the afternoon helping me get the house and yard fixed up."

"He's a very nice man," she added, "but because he's so old he sometimes forgets things. He left his false teeth in a glass of water in the sink," she said, laughing.

Charley asked, "What else has been going on?"

"Going on?" his mom asked, perplexed. "I don't know

what you mean. I just came up here to bring you and your friend, Otto, something to snack on. What's the matter, Charley? Is anything wrong?"

Charley said, "Chrissy had a weird look and green slimy stuff on her face. Dad's shirt was streaked with the same green slime. What was that stuff? I have to know!"

"Oh, that was just the green pea soup I made for Chrissy because she has a cold and isn't feeling well. And you know how much your dad loves green pea soup. I think he had two bowls just by himself although some of it dripped on his shirt."

"The green slime was just green pea soup?" Otto said, amazed.

"What did you think it was?"

"We thought it was the Creep," said Charley.

Charley's mom seemed surprised.

"I don't think you want to hear about it, mom. Believe me."

"Well," she said, "I have to go back downstairs and clean up the kitchen. And later, I'll bring you both a couple of bowls of soup. Green pea soup"

No one saw it, but a ball rolled quietly across the attic floor.

"When you are done with the soup, come down to the kitchen for the rest of your supper—I cooked up some wonderful liver I found in the refrigerator!"

Charley and Otto just looked at each other.

Then they screamed. *"The Creeeeeeep!"*

***

Charley and Otto heard something like water falling hard

from a storm. Outside the window, however, there was no rain. The water continued falling, falling hard.

"Listen!" said Charley.

"I hear it," Otto said. "It's water or something but where is it coming from?"

There was a bathroom at the end of the hall and the sound of the pouring water seemed to be coming from behind its closed door.

Steam was seeping out from under the door.

Charley and his friend moved toward the door. Finally, Charley turned the door handle. The door swung open and steam rushed out of the bathroom, covering them. They were sweating from the heat but Charley forced himself into the room. Not only was the bathroom hot with clouds of steam, it was dark and loud with crashing water. Charley switched on the light. Hot water was shooting out of the shower head, filling the bathtub. As the hot, steamy air escaped pass the open bathroom door, Charley and Otto saw that no one was in the room.

Otto reached for the shower handle and shut off the water.

"Maybe someone turned on the shower and forgot to turn it off," Charley said.

"No," Otto replied. "That just does not make sense."

"Then what could have caused the shower to turn on like that?" Charley wondered out loud.

"I have no idea," said Otto, "but I want to get out of here."

"Me, too," said Charley.

But as Charley and Otto turned away from the shower to leave the bathroom they noticed something written on the steamed-up mirror over the bathroom sink. In large, sprawling letters, someone—or something—had scrawled the words:

STAY AWAY FROM THE TV IN THE ATTIC!!!

CHAPTER 23

On a quiet moon-lit night, far on the edge of town, a strange long black car slowly moved along a dark street where no houses stood. The car moved slowly, rumbling and shaking, until it got to the top of a hill where the surface of a clear lake mirrored below. A red flame breathed out from beneath the strange car's old iron bones and then the long black car just sat there in the middle of the street, its image reflecting on the cold surface of the lake's water. No one was there to see the black car with its shiny chrome grill full of pointed rows of metal, sharp as sharks' teeth or the faint outline of the ghost-like driver behind the steering wheel.

After several minutes, the driver's side door opened. A

long thin arm followed by two longer legs and a tall body wearing a dark suit slid out from behind the steering wheel and stood alongside the car under the moon-lit night sky.

The faint murmur of lake water lapped against the shore at the bottom of the hill. The tall, thin man in the dark suit held something in his large hairy hand. The hairy hand squeezed the object a couple of times. When he opened his palm, there was a small rubber ball. The strange man called softly towards the lake, then waited. His eyes scanned the lake's surface, as if expecting something to appear in the water. He squeezed the ball again and once more he called into the moon-lit night, towards the lake water. Again he bounced the ball on the smooth road. He saw something large and greenish in the moonlight, rising from the lake's surface. The tall man in the dark suit squeezed the ball one more time, then threw it towards the lake before getting back into the strange black car and slowly driving down the road again, leaving behind a haunting trail of smoke. And as the car was disappearing into the night, somewhere a ghost dog was howling.

EPILOGUE

So there we have it, my dear friend—the story of a family who hoped to get away from the craziness of the big city and settle down in a nice, small town where they thought everything would go just dandy. And everything seemed to go just dandy—just dandy, that is, until Mr. C. Chills Wills showed up at their door to sell them a whole menu of cable TV channels.

Now, of course, you can't blame young Charley Nickels for wanting The Monster Chanel. Everyone seems to like monster movies. And you can't really blame it all on Mr. C. Chills Wills if you want to be perfectly honest, now can you? I mean, after all, C. Chills Wills did warn the boy but young Charley just wouldn't listen. Tsk, tsk, a shame that in the end Charley and his friend, Otto, were scared out of their wits—but I dare say it was all for the best, for now Charley and Otto will spend more time doing homework and playing in the fresh outdoors instead of sitting in front of the TV for hours on end and turning into unhealthy, corpulent coach potatoes!

As for our friend, Mr. C. Chills Wills, he continues to make cable TV sales for the Morgue Cable Company—he's quite the loyal employee—though I doubt he'll let the next kid talk him into getting The Monster Channel, well, at least not until the cable TV company works the kinks out of that monstrous TV station. I mean, we both understand, now don't we, that The Monster Channel as it currently is needs some rather fine-tuning before it's ready for the next family with a kid like Charley who no doubt will be moving into this wonderful town of Graves Lakes Estates—a place where anything can happen—and will—especially when you least expect it!

Oh, yes, our real estate professionals are getting phone calls and mail from other families who want to escape the big city and relocate to this wonderful little town tucked away from all the craziness of the world. After all, who can resist moving to such a wonderful little town where everything seems so picture perfect!

ABOUT THE AUTHOR

Jim Simon is a professional writer. He has written novels and nonfiction books, including work for Marvel Entertainment, DC Entertainment, Titan Publishing, and Abrams ComicArts. He appeared in the television movie/documentary, *Marvel's Captain America: 75 Heroic Years*. After writing *The Monster Channel*, he cancelled his cable TV.